THE NAUGHTY, THE NICE AND THE NANNY

WILLA NASH

THE NAUGHTY, THE NICE AND THE NANNY

ISBN: 978-1-950692-90-3

Editing & Proofreading:

Marion Archer, Making Manuscripts

www.makingmanuscripts.com

Julie Deaton, Deaton Author Services

www.facebook.com/jdproofs

Karen Lawson, The Proof is in the Reading

Judy Zweifel, Judy's Proofreading

www.judysproofreading.com

Cover:

OTHER TITLES

Calamity Montana Series

The Bribe

The Bluff

The Brazen

The Bully

Holiday Brothers Series

The Naughty, The Nice and The Nanny

Three Bells, Two Bows and One Brother's Best Friend

A Partridge and a Pregnancy

———

Writing as Devney Perry

Jamison Valley Series

The Coppersmith Farmhouse

The Clover Chapel

The Lucky Heart

The Outpost

The Bitterroot Inn

The Candle Palace

Maysen Jar Series

The Birthday List

Letters to Molly

Lark Cove Series

Tattered

Timid

Tragic

Tinsel

Clifton Forge Series

Steel King

Riven Knight

Stone Princess

Noble Prince

Fallen Jester

Tin Queen

Runaway Series

Runaway Road

Wild Highway

Quarter Miles

Forsaken Trail

Dotted Lines

The Edens Series

Christmas in Quincy - Prequel

Indigo Ridge

Juniper Hill

To Natasha Madison.
For your encouragement. For your laugh.
For your love of all things Christmas.

CHAPTER ONE

NATALIE

"She's an angel."

"Aren't they all?" I deadpanned.

"Of course not," my boss muttered on the other end of our phone call. "Some kids are shitheads."

"Whoa." I giggled. "Cathy."

"Natalie, I know you're on vacation, and I know you're overdue for a break, but you're the only one available to take this job. You know I hate turning down clients."

I scrunched up my nose. Cathy hated turning down clients, and I hated turning down Cathy. But this was my vacation. The first vacation I'd had in ages, and one I'd purposefully timed to coincide with Christmas.

I was going to enjoy the holidays with my own family instead of caring for someone else's.

This morning I'd come downtown for a hearty breakfast of eggs and pancakes at Main Street Overeasy before setting out to do some last-minute gift shopping while enjoying the festive décor.

Enormous gold, red and green garlands were strung high across the road, their strands twinkling beneath the clear blue sky. The trees, wrapped in tiny lights, glittered from last night's snow. Window displays were teeming with Santas, ornaments and intricately wrapped gifts. The morning sun was out, bright and cheery, warding off the winter chill. It was the perfect kickoff to my vacation.

"Cathy, I can't."

"Please," she begged. "The father sounded desperate. He's in town for the holidays. Sounded like the workaholic type. You'll be caring for his daughter during the day while he works. He mentioned a family holiday function as well, though I told him you were only obligated to work during the day. Apparently, his regular nanny walked out yesterday."

"I thought you said this girl was an angel. Nannies don't walk out on angels."

"He agreed to pay twice your regular rate."

I groaned. Of course, she'd tempt me with the money. "I never should have told you about Magdalena."

My beloved 1969 mint-green Volkswagen bus. Magdalena. Three weeks ago, her transmission had crapped out. The mechanic had ordered a new one from a parts store online that specialized in vintage Volkswagen parts, but with shipping, it was going to cost me over four thousand dollars.

I was a governess not a gazillionaire.

"And it's only for a week?" I asked.

"Yes. Just a week."

"Oh, stop your smiling. I asked a question. I didn't agree."

"How can you tell I'm smiling?"

I rolled my eyes. "You always smile when you get your way."

"So that's a yes?"

"Yes," I grumbled. "I'll do it."

"Excellent! Thank you. I'm sure this week will be a breeze." Cathy's famous last words.

She knew I preferred to work on long-term assignments. I'd been with my last family for three and a half years. The Scullys had been the best of the best family in Bozeman, Montana. Their kids were actual angels, sent from heaven to reward me for being the person Cathy could call upon for these *breezy* assignments.

The Scully boys had turned fourteen and sixteen this past year. Both were active in school, playing football, basketball and running track. Now that the oldest had his driver's license and they went to the same school, they didn't need me to shuffle them around from point A to point B.

My last day with them had been yesterday, and I'd cried like a baby while hugging them goodbye. They'd teased me mercilessly for my blubbering, and even though

Instagram wasn't cool for kids these days, they'd promised to post a selfie every week as proof of life.

After New Year's, I'd be starting with another family. The kids were five and nine. Assuming we had a good vibe, I might be their nanny for years.

Short-term jobs, like the one she was pitching, were more like glorified babysitter gigs.

But for Magdalena, I'd be the babysitter.

"Send me the details," I said.

"Okay. They're expecting you by ten, so you'd better get going."

"Ten." My feet ground to a halt. "Today? I thought you'd at least give me one day off. Can I start tomorrow?"

"Um . . ."

"It's three days before Christmas. I haven't finished my shopping yet." Because I'd blocked off my vacation days to buy and wrap gifts. "You're killing me, Cath."

"The mall is open until nine."

"You know I hate the mall," I muttered.

This served me right for putting off my shopping. Every year I swore I'd start earlier. And every year, I procrastinated. The mall this close to Christmas Eve was a particularly sweltering level of hell.

"Thank you, Natalie. I can always count on you."

"If it wasn't for Magdalena . . ."

She was smiling again. I could practically hear the stretch of her lips. "You're the best."

"You'd better pick me as Employee of the Year."

"You were Employee of the Year last year. Everyone will think I'm playing favorites."

"Because I am your favorite and you do play favorites."

"True."

"Bye." I ended the call and checked the time.

Ten o'clock was in twenty minutes.

I spun around, retreating to my dad's Subaru parked in one of the lots off Main. He'd loaned it to me while Magdalena was in the shop.

Dad always said I was fiercely loyal. At the moment, I felt epically spineless. Cathy might believe she had no one else to call, but that was because she always called me first. For short-term engagements like this, when my primary family was on vacation, or for a weekend when a client needed additional help, I was usually her first request. And I'd always said yes.

But she'd earned my devotion by treating me right over the years and giving me the best families, like the Scullys.

Cathy owned a local nanny agency in Bozeman, and with the growing online services available to parents these days, she survived by setting herself and her staff apart. We were not the caliber of nannies you'd find scouring the classifieds. Our reputation was unmatched and new clientele was sent through referrals only, hence the reason she hated to tell a prospect no.

This dad in desperate need of a holiday nanny for his *angel* probably hadn't blinked twice at a double-rate fee.

Magdalena, baby, this one is for you.

I reached the Subaru—*Barney? Barley?*—I was still in the process of picking the perfect name. My reflection in the car window had me whipping out my phone to call Cathy.

"If you're telling me you've changed your mind, you're too late," she answered. "I already called the father back and told him you were on the way."

"I don't have time to go home and change. Is there a dress code?"

"No dress code, but what are you wearing?"

"Blue turtleneck sweater. Ripped jeans. Duck boots." I was dressed for a day of shopping, not working. The Scullys hadn't had a dress code, but I never would have showed up in jeans with frayed knees. "I also haven't washed my hair yet."

"I'm sure it will be fine. I'll email him a note, letting him know that we've interrupted a personal day. If he has specific requests, he can let you know before tomorrow."

"Okay. Bye." I unlocked the car and got behind the wheel just as a text dinged from Cathy with the address. I punched it into my phone, then followed the GPS across town.

I'd lived in Bozeman for all of my twenty-nine years, and the fall after graduating from high school, I'd started working for Cathy.

As one of the fastest-growing cities in the country, Bozeman had transformed before my eyes and was no longer the town of my youth. Where there'd once been farmland, there were neighborhoods packed with new homes. Big-box stores were chasing out the small, local shops, and the number of new restaurants was staggering.

The directions took me to the outskirts of town, where the homes got larger and larger with every passing mile. As the mountain foothills neared, the properties sprawled and every private drive was blockaded by an iron gate.

"In one hundred yards, your destination is on the left." The navigation rang through the Subaru's Bluetooth.

Magdalena was too old for Bluetooth. I'd miss it—and these heated leather seats—when I returned the Subaru.

A log archway towered over the upcoming driveway entrance. The black metal gates were open as I eased onto a narrow lane lined with evergreens. Their limbs hid most of the house from sight until I rounded a gentle corner and then—*whoa*.

"Oh, hell. I definitely should have washed my hair."

It was a ski lodge masquerading as a family home.

With its dark wooden siding and red-trimmed windows, the house stood as proud and bold as the mountains at its back. The front door was wooden with a stained-glass window in its face. Where most porches would have a standard light, this home had two roaring gas lanterns, their flames flickering even during the day.

I'd been to many wealthy homes in my tenure as a nanny to Bozeman's elite but this one was the pinnacle. If Kevin Costner walked through the door and told me to get off the Dutton Ranch, I wouldn't be surprised. Only this wasn't the *Yellowstone* TV series, and as the clock on the dash glowed ten after ten, it was time for me to get to work.

Parking in the looped driveway that I suspected was for guests, I swiped up my purse from the passenger seat and checked my hair in the rearview. The blond waves I'd added this morning made my ponytail fancy—sort of.

The kid wouldn't care what I looked like, right? And the father, well . . . he'd have to deal with short-notice Natalie.

I stepped outside and hurried to the house, pressing the doorbell. Its chime was a familiar tune. Was that . . .

"We Wish You a Merry Christmas." I gave the door my best lip curl. That stupid song would be stuck in my head all damn day.

Footsteps sounded from inside and I put on my smile, ready to greet my new employer. The door flew open and—

"Hi—oh." My. God. Oh my God. Oh my God.

I'd just said *hi-oh* like one of Snow White's singing dwarves to Maddox Holiday.

The Maddox Holiday. The handsome boy turned *holy-shit-he-was-hot* man who'd once occupied each and every one of my teenage fantasies.

Maddox Holiday.

He'd been the most popular guy at Bozeman High. He'd been the boy every girl had shamelessly crushed on. He was the rich dad in need of an emergency nanny?

I definitely should have asked more questions before agreeing to this. I definitely should have washed my hair.

"Hi. Are you from Cathy Caron's agency?"

"Yes. Hi." I managed it without the oh. *Better.* "I'm Natalie Buchanan."

"Maddox Holiday." He waved me inside and closed the door behind us. "Nice to meet you, Natalie."

Wait. Nice to meet me? Seriously?

He'd already met me.

When. I. Was. Seven.

I stepped past him, wishing, hoping and praying that there'd be a faint flicker of recognition in his mesmerizing blue gaze. But . . . nothing.

The guy had no clue who I was. *Damn.*

Maddox was three years older than me, so it wasn't like we'd run in the same circles. But for many years, we'd gone to the same schools. His twin brothers were my age. He should know me.

Still . . . nothing.

Fourteen-year-old me died a little inside. Her fantasy that one day Maddox Holiday would realize she was the love of his life went *poof* like a tuft of snow in the wind.

What was I doing here? When was I going to learn to tell Cathy no? For the next week, Maddox Holiday would essentially be my boss. And the man didn't have a clue that I'd once fallen off my skateboard and scraped my knee in his driveway.

"Thanks for coming on such short notice," he said.

"Sure." More wishing. More hoping. More praying.

Nope. Nada. He didn't recognize me.

Captain's log. December twenty-second. Today marks the most humiliating day of my life.

Should I tell him? Would that make it weird? Probably.

Magdalena was counting on me to rescue her from the mechanic, so I squared my shoulders, put on a smile and pretended that I was standing across from any other father who was paying me to care for his child.

"Did Cathy explain the position?" he asked.

"At the highest level." Though she'd left out his name, one I would have remembered. I suspected the full details about this position were in my email inbox. "You need a nanny for a week, correct?"

"A week. Your predecessor walked out yesterday." His jaw clenched, and *wowza*, it was chiseled. The corners were so sharp they deserved a snowman statue in their honor.

Just another dad. He's just another dad.

Okay, so maybe he wasn't exactly like other dads. None of the fathers I'd worked for in recent years were this insanely handsome. None had eyes like crystal-blue jewels. None had a gravelly voice that sent shivers down my spine.

Time had only improved Maddox Holiday.

He seemed taller now, standing a head over my five-foot eight. Maddox's face was clean-shaven, and his dark hair had been finger-combed away from his face. In high school, he'd kept his hair short, but if he would have had this hair, he would have had girls shoving their panties in his locker.

He probably already had.

Breathe, Natalie. It's just Maddox mega-hot Holiday. Focus on work. The job. The kid. "You have a daughter, correct?"

"I do. Violet." His gaze softened at his daughter's name. "She's seven. We're home for the holidays to visit my parents. This is their house, so I'm afraid there's never a quiet moment."

"Oh. Okay." The ski lodge belonged to Hannah and Keith? I wasn't sure why I was surprised. The Holidays were one of the most successful families in Bozeman.

Hannah was a real estate broker, and her face was on at least half of the for-sale signs around town. Her brokerage was the most well-known and most respected in the county, partly because she sold the best homes—those her husband built.

Keith Holiday was the most sought-after custom-home builder in the area. People paid a premium for a Holiday Home and were never disappointed.

Keith must have built this place. Even though I'd only seen the foyer, the interior was as grand and gorgeous as the exterior. A chandelier hung high above my head, its pendants refracting the light. Sunshine poured through the abundance of windows. The natural stone tiles beneath my boots were a beautiful shade of grayish blue.

It would not be hard to work in this house for a week.

When Maddox and his brothers had been growing up, they'd lived in town. Two blocks over from my house.

Heath and Tobias used to ride their bikes past my childhood home on their way to our neighborhood park.

Wait. His brothers. Maddox might not remember me, but Heath and Tobias would. Were they going to be here?

"Is that okay?" Maddox asked.

"Huh?"

"You look worried." He studied my face, his eyes narrowing. "The extra people in and out. Will that be a problem?"

"Not a problem," I lied, fixing my smile.

"Good. I wish I had the week off work, but it's a critical time for my company. I'll be working in the house, upstairs in the office, in case anything comes up. But with the phone conferences and emails—"

"Adding a seven-year-old into the mix is too much."

"Exactly." He nodded. "I just need some help. My parents would normally jump in and watch her, but they're busy planning the annual party on Christmas Eve. Plus they're working this week too. I don't want Violet bouncing between us all, feeling lost. I want her to have some fun while we're here."

That was sweet. Then again, Maddox had always been sweet. It was the reason all the girls had crushed on him. He'd never let his popularity or good looks turn him into the arrogant playboy like so many other guys in his social circle.

"And Violet's mother?" I asked. Maddox hadn't mentioned a wife and there was no ring on his left hand. "Will she be here?"

"No, I'm divorced. She's in LA."

"Okay." Single dad. Grown-up Maddox just kept getting sexier.

"I'll let Violet give you the tour of the place. But please make yourself comfortable while you're here." Maddox studied me and for a moment my heart swelled. Did he remember me? Yes? Please? "Violet is probably in her room."

Gah. This guy sure knew how to crush a girl's ego. Not that I had an ego. Geeks who loved board games and volunteering at the senior center to call the Sunday bingo games couldn't afford egos.

While Maddox had been dominating the football field as quarterback and dating the head cheerleader, I'd spent my Friday nights in high school babysitting for the neighbors.

"Thank you again for coming." Maddox gave me a small smile that crinkled his eyes. Another improvement of man over boy. Except beneath the smile and rugged good looks, he looked . . . tired. I'd seen that type of exhaustion before in a lot of parents who'd brought in a nanny to help. Mostly it had been from mothers and fathers with demanding jobs who'd realized they couldn't do it all.

Natalie to the rescue.

"You're welcome. It'll be my pleasure. Cathy said she is an angel."

A flash of panic crossed his gaze. It was as telling as the previous nanny's hasty departure. "Let's, uh . . . let's go find Violet."

I followed him as he walked deeper into the house, doing my best not to stare at his firm ass in the best pair of jeans I'd seen in my life. His long legs moved with a natural swagger, the kind that most attractive men must have been taught in college.

Maddox glanced over his shoulder.

I tore my eyes away, barely in time, before he busted me staring at his behind. "It's a beautiful house."

Smooth, Natalie. Really smooth.

"My dad built it."

I forced my gaze to the house and off the man. "He did a fantastic job."

The walls were painted a soft white. The decorative wood accents gave the tall, open spaces warmth. The windows were a feature on their own, providing views at every angle of the sprawling snow-covered property beyond the glass.

Maddox led me past a living room full of cozy leather pieces. Red embers glowed in the stone fireplace. Past the hearth, a sweeping staircase with a beautiful, spindled railing led to the second floor.

"I'll get you the gate code for tomorrow morning in case it's closed," Maddox said, glancing over his shoulder as we started up the steps.

"I parked in the front loop. Is that okay or would you prefer I park in a different spot?"

"The front is fine. Mom hired a chef for the week so there's no need to cook for Violet. If you have any dietary restrictions, just let him know."

"None unless vegetables count. I trade vegetables for Christmas cookies this time of year."

Maddox chuckled and the smile that stretched across his face nearly sent me careening over the banister. Straight white teeth. Full lips. A dimple. I'd forgotten about that dimple over the years.

Boss. He's my boss-ish. Which was why I only stared at his ass for three stairs instead of five. In my defense, it was at eye level.

The second floor was as beautiful as the first. At the top of the stairs, a balcony overlooked the living room. Plush carpets padded our footsteps as we walked down a hallway.

Maddox stopped at the third door. "Violet?"

The bedroom was bigger than my living room. A fluffy, white bed sat in the center of the room, draped with a gauze canopy. The toy chest against the wall was open and the floor littered with books and stuffed animals and . . . was that a Nerf gun?

Excellent. I'd expected Barbies but Nerf guns were much better. After years with boys, I'd become a self-proclaimed sharpshooter.

"Violet," Maddox called again.

No answer.

"She was just in here." His forehead furrowed. "Violet, if you're hiding, please come out."

Silence.

"Violet." He marched into the en suite bathroom, coming out seconds later to check under the bed. "Maybe she went to the kitchen."

I followed as he led the way to the main floor. We'd just reached the living room when a crash echoed through the house.

"Shit." Maddox's steps hastened down one more hallway.

The scent of sugar and vanilla hit my nose. Cake. Or cookies, but I was guessing cake. When it came to sweets, I was also a self-proclaimed expert.

We rounded a corner and stepped into a wide kitchen I suspected most restaurateurs would drool over. Standing in front of a cluttered island, a red-faced man in a chef's coat was wiping a glob of chocolate cake batter off his neck.

His nostrils flared. His gaze was narrowed on a girl in the middle of the room.

She wore a red tutu and matching glitter slippers. In one hand, she held a wooden spoon. In the other, a butcher's knife.

"You must be Violet," I said.

The angel.

CHAPTER TWO

MADDOX

"Hey." Heath strolled into my office. Without knocking. Did he not see me on the phone?

I held up a finger as he plopped into a leather chair in the corner of the room.

"Let me know after you talk to the owner," I told my assistant. "I'm willing to sign a seven-year lease, but I'd prefer five. Push for that."

"You got it."

"Thanks, John. Have a merry Christmas."

"Same to you, Maddox."

I ended the call and pinched the bridge of my nose. This headache wasn't going away, even after two aspirin and a jug of water. The throb had bloomed beneath my temples at exactly the same time I'd found Violet in the kitchen.

With a goddamn knife.

After hours of endless calls and back-to-back meetings, the pain had only grown. It was rare that I came to Montana, and the last thing I wanted to do was spend my vacation working. But there were tasks to be done. Too much work to finish if I was actually going to move here.

I was in the middle of determining where and when I could set up a satellite office for my company. The employees who'd been open to a move to Montana would need a work space. Then there was building a house for Violet and me.

If it all came together, soon, Montana wouldn't just be a vacation destination. It would be home.

And instead of bothering me with endless texts and phone calls, my brothers would be able to interrupt my day in person.

"What do you want?" I barked at Heath.

"Someone's in the holiday spirit."

I shot him a glare. "Seriously. I have a million things to do before I'm done today. State your business."

"Did you ask him?" Tobias strolled into the room with a stack of cookies in his hand. Again, without a knock.

"Give me one of those."

"Say please."

"Please." I snapped my fingers. "Now."

"You're in a mood today." Tobias crossed the room and handed over a chocolate crinkle.

"I have a headache, and today's been a train wreck." I sighed, taking a bite of the cookie, hoping some sugar would improve my outlook. Was it too early for a drink? One o'clock was, well . . . one o'clock. Technically, I was on vacation.

"What's going on?" Heath asked.

"I'm having a hell of a time finding office space that's big enough, nice enough and an owner who doesn't think that because he googled my net worth, I'm willing to pay LA prices in Montana."

I'd made the initial calls myself, but after the third property owner had quoted me an exorbitant price, I'd delegated the task to John.

"The nanny I'd brought with me from LA decided to quit and enjoy a nice holiday vacation this week. After I flew her up here in my jet. Oh, and this morning I found my daughter in the kitchen with a knife."

"That's why we're here." Tobias took the matching leather chair beside Heath's. The look the twins shared had me sitting straighter.

"What?"

"When did you hire Natalie Buchanan?"

I blinked. "The nanny?"

"Told you he didn't recognize her." Heath swiped a cookie from Tobias's hand, chomping on the gingersnap. "Natalie Buchanan. She was in our class. Nice but sort of nerdy back then."

She had looked familiar, with blue eyes that had instantly drawn me in. But I'd been too busy trying not to stare at her long, slender legs to place her face.

"Definitely not nerdy now," Tobias said. "I haven't seen her in ages. She looks good."

Good was one word. Beautiful was another. But she was my employee and there was no way I would make that comment aloud.

"Leave her alone," I ordered. "She's here to watch Violet. I'm out of options so unless you want to be saddled with babysitting your niece for the next week, don't bother Natalie."

"Babysit Violet? Oh, hell no." Heath shot out of his chair and, as quickly as he'd come into the office, he disappeared.

"What was that supposed to mean?"

Tobias's gaze dropped to the floor. Then, like Heath, Tobias scurried away too.

So maybe Violet wasn't exactly an easygoing child. She wasn't a typical girl either, one who played with dollhouses and Barbies and makeup—assuming that's what other seven-year-old girls did. Besides Violet, I didn't have experience with other children.

Hence the nannies.

A whole fucking string of nannies.

Not even professionals seemed to have the capacity to handle my daughter. If Natalie survived the week, I'd be impressed.

In the past year, I'd had thirty-two nannies. The longest had stayed with us for seven weeks, probably because I'd scaled down her duties significantly. All she'd had to do was walk Violet to school in the morning, pick her up each afternoon, then spend three hours with her until I'd come home at six.

Apparently, three hours had been too much because on the day she'd quit, the woman had filled twenty minutes telling me everything that was wrong with my child.

Spoiled.

Unruly.

Naughty.

Not a single nanny out of thirty-two had enjoyed spending time with my daughter. It was like taking that goddamn butcher's knife she'd had this morning to the heart.

Violet was . . . difficult. The divorce had taken its toll. She acted out more often than normal. I wasn't blind or deaf to her antics. I just didn't know how to fix it.

Hopefully moving to Montana would be part of the answer.

But we weren't here yet. And at the moment, I simply wanted to survive Christmas unscathed. With any luck, Natalie could stick it out with Violet, at least through Mom and Dad's party. Once the party was over on Christmas Eve, Mom would have more free time to pitch in. At this point, if Natalie made it through today before she quit, I'd take it.

She was probably going to quit.

Natalie Buchanan.

Huh. Out of context, I hadn't recognized her name. She'd been the nanny from the agency, nothing more. I preferred using agencies because they did all the necessary background checks to vet caregivers before they came into my home, and after thirty-two nannies, the names had begun to blur.

But now that Heath and Tobias had pointed out who she was, I felt like a fool for missing it. Why hadn't she told me?

I shoved away from my desk, knowing I didn't have time for anything but work and Violet, but I took a minute anyway. Mom kept all our old yearbooks in this office, organized by year on the bottom row of a bookshelf. I plucked my senior yearbook out and brought it back to my desk.

The spine cracked as I flipped it open. The pages smelled like my senior year—football fields and keggers and sweet anticipation for the future. As I scanned the pages, I let myself be eighteen again. I forgot the burdens of a thirty-two-year-old single father and escaped to a time when my biggest worries were next week's game and my upcoming calculus exam.

The pages turned heavily, clinging to each other like magnets. The stupid smile on my face spread as I got deeper into the book, seeing group photos and club activities, all captured on the pages.

Then there she was. Standing in the back row of a

group photo for the ten-person swim team. *Natalie Buchanan.*

Yeah, I definitely should have remembered her. She was a woman now, but her blond hair was the same, and so were her eyes. The pretty blues stood out from the photo, an electric color like the bulbs Mom had strung on the mini-Christmas tree in my bedroom.

Every room in the house had a tree, each with varying colors of lights and decorations. It would take her a month to stow it away. Each year she'd cuss and promise never to do so much decorating, but each year after Thanksgiving, she'd send me pictures of the trees, one by one as she put them up.

Tonight when I went to sleep, that tree's glow would make me think of Natalie.

Exactly the wrong person to think of when I was in bed.

Natalie Buchanan.

Damn, but she did look good. As a teenager, she'd been cute. As a grown woman, she was a stunner. I took another long look at her smile in the club photo, then flipped to the sophomore section and found her picture.

She was wearing a black turtleneck, the exact opposite of what the girls I'd dated had worn back then. They'd all pushed the boundaries of the school's dress code, seeing just how low those V-necks could stretch before getting called into the principal's office.

Natalie's hair was different in this picture than in the

swim-team photo. She had bangs that nearly covered her eyebrows and were chopped in a harsh, straight line. Her smile looked wobbly and her eyes were squinted.

Bless those school photographers. They had a true talent for bringing out every teenager's inner awkward.

My phone rang, pulling me away from the yearbook. I set it aside and fit my earbuds into my ears before diving back into my workday. Jumping from call to call, I spent the next few hours giving my team rapid-fire instructions and hoping that if I delegated enough, I could take at least one day off during this trip. At the very least, not spend my evenings answering emails.

My mother would string me up with my blue Christmas tree lights if I missed a dinner. Not just because Violet was the world's pickiest eater, but because I hadn't seen my parents enough these past seven years. Once we moved here, we'd be making up for lost time.

For all of us. I'd missed my parents and my brothers. And I wanted them to have a stronger bond with my daughter.

But first, I needed a place to live.

Yesterday, I'd put an offer on a lot outside of town. It was fifty acres, giving me plenty of space between neighbors and lots of room for Violet to roam. There was a pond and direct access to a secluded mountain hiking trail.

The moment I'd seen it, even covered in snow, I'd jumped.

Dad and I had stayed up late last night discussing

possibilities for a floor plan. As soon as I had the property, he'd pull some strings to get a crew over and break ground.

"What did they counter with?" I asked my realtor. This was our second conversation today.

"They want full ask."

"Of course, they do," I grumbled.

Dollar signs had likely flashed in their eyes at my name. But I hadn't made over a billion dollars by letting people push me into unfair prices. "Offer it. Remind their realtor this is a cash offer with a short close. If they squabble about anything, I'll walk. There are plenty of parcels in the Gallatin Valley these days."

Even though this was the one I wanted.

"Exactly," she said. "This is a smart move, Maddox. Really brilliant."

I rolled my eyes. She worked for Mom's company and had been a major kiss ass. But she was getting the job done so I'd been ignoring her over-the-top compliments. If not for the super-sweet sugary tone, her compliment probably wouldn't have bothered me at all. I was used to it.

Cece had perfected that tone years ago. She'd use it right before dropping a bomb in my lap.

"Email me a list of other options, just in case."

"Of course."

"Thanks." I ended the call and set my phone aside.

My stomach growled and another cookie beckoned.

Time for a break. I rubbed the nape of my neck, trying to work out what felt like a permanent knot, then picked up the yearbook and returned it to Mom's shelf. But before I walked away, curiosity got the better of me. I pulled out Heath and Tobias's senior year album, flipping through the pages.

And there she was again, on another swim-team photo.

Natalie's bangs had disappeared on her journey from freshman to senior. She was in the back row, standing amongst the boys. She was taller than the other girls, something I'd noticed earlier.

I was six-three, and most women I knew, other than Mom, had to crane their necks to meet my gaze. Not Natalie.

She wore a simple one-piece suit in the photo. In the freshman team picture, they'd all been in matching sweats and hoodies. But this swimsuit . . .

It all clicked into place.

"Damn." I chuckled. Yeah, I remembered Natalie.

I hadn't spent a lot of time by the pool at our high school, but for a few weeks during senior year, the normal entrance to our locker rooms had been closed. Before football practice, we'd had to use the swim side entrance.

One day when I'd gone through, Natalie had been in the pool. As I'd walked by, she'd shoved up and out of the water and no straight seventeen-year-old boy would have passed her without a double take.

Trim figure. Lush breasts. Taut nipples from the cold air. She'd been in a black swim cap, probably to protect those bangs from turning green. Why I remembered that cap I wasn't sure. Maybe because it shouldn't have been hot. But it was. *She* was.

And now she was basically an employee.

I slammed the book closed and shoved it back in the shelf. Then I squeezed my eyes shut to brandish the image of Natalie, my new nanny, out of my head.

Employee. Off-limits.

And this was not the time nor place to get twisted up by a woman. Dealing with Cece was enough of a migraine.

"Hey." Heath strode into the office, again without a knock. "What are you doing? You looked her up, didn't you?"

"Yeah." I stood and moved away from the bookshelf. "What are you doing?"

He lifted a shoulder. "Nothing today."

"Don't you have to work?"

"It's called vacation. V-A-C-A-T-I-O-N. Ever heard of it?"

"Vaguely." I sighed and took one of the leather chairs.

Heath took the seat next to mine, bringing the coffee mug he'd brought to his lips. "The chef made Tom and Jerrys."

"Later. Still have some work to do." My phone vibrated in my pocket and I took it out to see a text from the realtor. The sellers had accepted my offer on the lot. "Looks like I've got property in Montana."

"Nice. That place with the pond?"

"Yeah. Cost a fortune."

"You can afford it. Dad and I talked today. I'm going to run lead on your build, if that's okay with you."

I nodded. "You bet."

Both Heath and Tobias worked for Dad's company. Heath oversaw the actual builds. Tobias was an architect. The twins had inherited our father's talent for design and management, and one day, they'd take over as owners of Holiday Homes.

"Mom was gossiping earlier about Cece," he said.

"Oh, hell." I groaned. "What now?"

My mother hated my ex-wife, something she didn't try to hide from anyone but Violet.

"Cece posted some selfie on Instagram from a beach."

"Sounds like Cece." I'd had to unfollow my ex because seeing her jaunting around the globe on my dime while missing weekends with Violet had made me homicidal.

Part of what made this move to Montana so appealing was that Bozeman was thousands of miles away from the city and Cece.

After the divorce three years ago, I'd stayed in LA. Partly for work. Partly with hope that Cece would decide to become a mother. Clearly, I'd been delusional.

Cece cared about Cece and Cece alone.

Violet needed more than me and a parade of nannies. She needed family. My family. She needed consistent affection from grandparents. Teasing and horsing around with her uncles.

Mom and Dad were over the moon that we were moving home. My brothers were wary of Violet at the moment, but eventually they'd warm up to her. If I was raising Violet alone, I was doing it in Montana, and Cece couldn't do a damn thing about it. Not anymore.

She cared more about her divorce settlement than our daughter.

The two of us had married young, a couple months after I'd graduated from college. When I'd made the announcement, Dad had pulled me aside and begged me to get a prenup. Luckily, I'd agreed.

When Keith Maddox gave advice, you were smart to listen.

Maybe he'd known I'd been destined for success. Maybe he'd seen Cece's true colors. Maybe both. Whatever the reason, we'd had one drawn up before our wedding. Cece hadn't liked it but she'd signed—something my attorney had reminded hers during the divorce negotiation.

I'd earned billions of dollars, and she hadn't been able to touch a penny.

But the prenup hadn't mattered. She'd had leverage. Violet.

What should have been a simple divorce had turned into a long, painful argument because I'd refused to give her part-time custody of our daughter. Cece had been a part-time parent to Violet, at best, while we'd been married. She'd also had the help of nannies, chefs and housekeepers. She didn't have the skill or the desire to care for our child.

But in the end, she'd won.

I agreed to pay her a ridiculous lump sum if she agreed to giving me full custody.

From that moment on, the divorce had moved like a hot knife through butter. Once the papers were signed, I'd said goodbye to my wife. And Violet had watched her mother disappear.

The nannies I'd hired couldn't fill a mother's shoes. I knew that. It had just been a bandage over a gushing wound, and it was time to get out the gauze and staunch the flow.

Mom would help. Montana would help too.

"Is Violet excited to move?" Heath asked.

"Not really. She's angry that she has to make new friends. She's mad that she has to start at a new school. Honestly, I don't blame her. But every damn time Cece lets her down, it gets harder. We have to get out of LA."

"She'll adjust. It's only second grade."

"Try telling that to Violet."

"Ha. I don't think so. No offense, Maddox, but your kid scares the shit out of me."

I chuckled. "When I brought Natalie in and gave her the quick tour, Violet was in the kitchen. She'd *accidentally* spilled a bowl of cake batter, and she'd gone for the chef's butcher knife so she could cut herself a piece of apple pie."

"I'm surprised Natalie didn't run for the door."

"Me too," I admitted.

Instead, she'd calmly crossed the room with a smile and taken the knife from Violet's hand, all while the chef had been ranting about his cake batter and I'd been struck dumbfounded.

"It's my fault," I told Heath. "I am sucking at this father gig."

"You've got a lot on your plate."

"Too much." I couldn't run my company in LA and be the full-time father Violet needed at the same time. It was time to offload some responsibilities to my staff. They could handle it.

The team I was hoping to bring to Montana were my elite. Each would get a considerable moving bonus and annual salary bump. They might have to tear some tasks out of my grasp—I'd warned them as such—but they were extremely capable.

Violet needed me more than Madcast.

We still had to return to LA after the holidays. I'd lined up a new nanny to start once we got back to LA. Hopefully my vivacious, beautiful daughter wouldn't send her racing for the door. But maybe once we actually moved to Bozeman, I wouldn't find a replacement. Maybe it could just be the two of us for a change.

Plus a chef because I was hopeless in the kitchen.

"Maybe I will have a Tom and Jerry. Are they good?" I asked my brother.

Heath answered by handing over his mug.

I took a sip, coughing at the burn. "Damn. That's got a kick."

"I already called dibs on a downstairs guest room tonight. No way I'm driving home after a few of these."

I stood, ready to hit the kitchen for a cocktail and another cookie, when a loud crash echoed through the house.

Heath shot to his feet.

I froze, waiting for the inevitable.

A loud gasp. A scream. A string of expletives.

Nothing came.

The house went eerily quiet, which only made my terror spike.

"Uh . . ." Heath looked to me.

I bolted out of the office, with Heath not far behind, rushing toward the balcony that overlooked the living room.

And there she was.

My beautiful girl.

Violet stood on top of the coffee table. Her arms were crossed over her chest. There was a scowl twisting her lips and the glare in her eyes was one I hoped she would use to keep boys away when she turned sixteen.

At the moment, that angry stare was aimed at the nanny.

Natalie's blond hair and blue sweater were dripping

with water. Shards of a shattered white vase were at her feet along with two dozen red roses.

Flowers that I'd ordered for my mother yesterday.

I didn't need to ask what had happened. My guess was that Violet had *accidentally* tipped that vase over Natalie's head.

"Violet," I hissed.

My daughter's eyes snapped up to mine. The scowl didn't disappear. She didn't even look sorry.

"See? She's terrifying," Heath whispered, putting his hand on my shoulder. "I'm locking my bedroom door tonight."

"You're not helping." I brushed off his touch and stormed down the stairs, unsure whether I was more embarrassed or furious. Mortification won out.

"Dad—"

"I'll discuss this with you later," I told my daughter, then focused on Natalie. "I'm so sorry. I'll pay you for the entire week. I'll contact the agency and make sure they understand that the reason this didn't work out was in no way your fault."

Natalie, who had been staring at Violet as I spoke, finally shifted her gaze. Those blue eyes met mine and the air rushed from my lungs. Not from the beauty of her face, but the smile that stretched across her mouth.

Though breathtaking, that smile was laced with malice. With revenge.

A wolf in a sexy nanny's body.

"Oh, I'm not leaving," she said, arching an eyebrow.

"You're not?"

"Nope." Natalie locked her own glare with Violet's, and in the space that separated them, the battle line was drawn.

Natalie reached for the hem of her sweater, dragging the soaked top off her body. Underneath she wore a thin white tank top that molded to her breasts and flat stomach. It was nearly as skintight as the wet swimsuit I'd seen her in years ago.

"Violet and I were just getting to know each other. Weren't we, Violet?"

Before my daughter could answer, Natalie rolled up her sweater, twisting it into a rope.

Then she raised her arms and wrung it out.

Over my daughter's head.

CHAPTER THREE

NATALIE

"How did yesterday go?" Cathy asked, her voice booming through the Subaru's speakers.

"Great," I lied. "She's a sweetie."

Violet was a tutu-toting terrorist, but there was no way in hell a seven-year-old girl was going to best me.

That little brat.

Violet and I had ended yesterday in war.

I was still a bit mystified at the kid's strength. She'd picked up that full vase, water and all, and had *accidentally* dumped it on me. It was a miracle I hadn't gotten a thorn in my eye.

She'd bested me yesterday. I'd give her the point. But today, I was coming prepared. That was . . . if I'd be allowed to watch her again. Maddox might banish me from his parents' home, and though I'd hate not seeing him again, I wouldn't be heartbroken. I'd find another way to pay for Magdalena's repairs.

After the red roses incident yesterday, he'd stared at me like he'd seen the Ghost of Christmas Past. Immediately after I'd wrung my turtleneck out over Violet's head, she'd stomped upstairs in a furious flurry. I'd managed to force a polite smile for Maddox, all too aware that my white camisole had left little to the imagination, then had followed his daughter, soggy sweater in hand.

When five o'clock had rolled around, he'd found us both at the small table in Violet's room. She'd been coloring in a Santa book, holding the crayons so fiercely she'd broken the entire collection of reds.

Maddox had offered to walk me to the door, but I'd told him I could find my own way out. Then with a saccharine-sweet farewell to Violet, I'd escaped to the safety of my own home where I'd had to watch *Home Alone* twice to improve my mood. If I did get fired today, I'd already queued up *The Polar Express* and a pint of ice cream.

"Did you hear anything from Mr. Holiday?" I asked. Like how I'd lost my temper and drenched his daughter in rose-stem water.

"Uh, no. Should I expect to?"

"Nope," I said, too brightly. "It's all good."

"Thanks again for doing this. I'm off tomorrow and Saturday for Christmas but you have my cell if you need anything."

"Will do. Merry Christmas."

"Merry Christmas."

I ended the call, continuing down the road and turning onto the Holidays' private lane. The house was as impressive today as it had been yesterday, and when I parked in the front loop, I took a moment to appreciate the details I'd missed yesterday. The copper gutters. The carved gables. The driveway—heated, judging by the lack of snow and wisps of steam rising from the black surface.

What would it be like to have that kind of money? I doubted I'd ever know and that was all right by me. I'd grown up in a normal, three-bedroom, two-bathroom home full of love and laughter. That was a currency of its own, and in that regard, I was a wealthy woman.

Not that the Holiday house wasn't full of love. Yesterday, I'd bumped into both Heath and Tobias. With Bozeman growing like it was and our social circles running in opposite directions, I hadn't seen either of them in years.

The twins, like Maddox, had grown from the lanky boys I'd remembered in high school to incredibly handsome men, though not quite as good-looking as their older brother.

I climbed out of Dad's car, instantly missing the heated seats. Barney or Barley was growing on me with his modern comforts. *I still love you, Magdalena. Always.*

My breath billowed in a cloud as I opened the back

door and retrieved my tote bag. The zipper bulged at the seam. This morning, I'd loaded every trick in my arsenal.

Bring it, Violet.

Squaring my shoulders, I headed for the porch, about to ring the bell when the heavy walnut door flung open and there he was.

Hello, Maddox Holiday.

Damn, but he was gorgeous.

"Morning," he said.

"Morning. Are you going to fire me?"

He laughed and that dazzling white smile with the dimple appeared. The flock of Christmas carolers who took up residence in a corner of my mind this time of year chorused, "Hal-le-lu-jah."

"Honestly, I'm in a bit of shock." He held the door for me as I stepped inside.

"So the jury's still out on me being fired?" I set my tote down to strip off my coat and hang it on a hook.

"No, shocked that you came back. Each one of your predecessors would have bailed."

"I'm not the bailing type. And today, I came prepared." I hefted up my bag and smacked its side.

"My parents are here today." Maddox led us to the living room. "I suspect my brothers will be around whenever their stomachs drive them here for sustenance. I'll be in the office most of the day but am available if you need anything."

"I'm sure we'll be fine. Where is Violet?" *Come out, come out, little one. It's time to play.*

Like she heard my silent summons, Violet trudged into the room. No tutu today. Instead she was wearing a pair of jeans and a fuzzy red sweater.

Red was most definitely her color, and not because there was a real possibility that she was Lucifer's spawn. It brought out the milk-chocolate strands in her long, brown hair. Her blue eyes popped, just like her father's. She'd be the most beautiful child in the world if not for that epic scowl.

We'd work on fixing that today.

"Hi, Violet." I smiled.

She glared.

I had to give this kid props. She was a formidable opponent, but I was not your typical nanny. I liked to think that Dad had raised me tougher than your average caretaker.

"Violet, Natalie said hello," Maddox said, a warning in his tone.

She crossed her arms over her chest and gave a harrumph.

Maddox's gaze, full of remorse, met mine.

"Don't worry." I winked. "We'll be fine."

"I can get my mom—"

"Nope." I cut him off when I saw a glint of hope in Violet's gaze. This was exactly what she wanted. "All good here. I'm here"—I locked eyes with Violet—"for the whole day. All. Day. Long."

Maddox looked between the two of us. "Um . . ."

"Should we head up to your room, Violet? I brought some things with me."

She glared at my bag. "What things?"

I didn't bother answering. I simply turned and walked to the staircase, my chin held high. When I heard the smack of her shoes on the wooden stairs behind me, I knew I'd won.

Maddox stared at us from the living room, his hands on his hips and a look of befuddlement on his handsome face.

Poor guy. His kid was walking all over him with those glitter slippers.

Yesterday, Violet had informed me that they were moving to Montana. She hadn't seemed happy about it. Maybe that was the reason for this attitude. Maybe it was Maddox's work schedule. Or maybe she was just used to getting her way.

Well, not with me. Not this week.

We reached the top of the stairs and headed down the hallway toward Violet's bedroom when a woman emerged from another room. I recognized Hannah Holiday immediately, not only from the plethora of real estate signs around town but from the woman I remembered cheering for her sons at high school football and basketball games.

She'd never once forgotten to bring an air horn.

"Oh, hello." She smiled. "You must be Natalie."

"I am." I smiled back. "We never formally met, but I graduated with Heath and Tobias."

"Yes, of course." Hannah nodded. "They told me last night. We had to get out the yearbooks."

"Ooof. Please tell me you didn't see evidence of the bang-pocalypse my sophomore year." And please tell me Maddox wasn't there too.

"That's an awkward age for everyone, dear."

I laughed as Violet stepped up to us, staring back and forth as we spoke.

Hannah touched her granddaughter's shoulder. "Baby, why don't you go get out something to play with while I visit with Natalie for a minute."

"But, Nana—"

"Off you go."

Violet frowned but obeyed.

When she disappeared into her bedroom, Hannah blew out a long breath. "That girl."

"She's got spirit."

"Ha!" Hannah laughed. "You're so polite."

"Who's polite?" Keith came striding our way from behind Hannah. He saluted me with his coffee cup. "Morning. You must be Natalie."

"Guilty."

"Good for you yesterday," he said. "I wish I would have been here to see it. Violet can be a little shi—"

"Keith." Hannah's elbow jabbed her husband's side.

"Hey." He frowned at his wife. "Sorry. What I meant to say was that Violet needs someone who will give her a dose of her own, er . . . sass."

"I might have gotten a little carried away."

He chuckled. "Nah."

"Okay." Hannah checked her watch, then looked to Keith. "We'd better get going. Our meeting is at nine and I want to swing by the office first."

"Every year I swear it's our last Christmas party and every year she convinces me to do it again." Keith sighed. "Good luck today, Natalie."

"Same to you." I smiled, then headed to Violet's room. No surprise, I caught her sprinting away from the doorway where she'd been eavesdropping. "I brought something for you."

"I don't want it." She plopped down at her desk and plucked a red marker from the pile. Then she began drawing.

On. The. Table.

Those markers were washable and it wouldn't take more than a wet cloth to clean the surface, but when her blue eyes flickered my way, I shrugged, feigning indifference as I went to the bed, sat down and unzipped my bag.

The contents were irresistible, even to the most difficult of children.

"Fine by me." I dug through the tote, shoving aside the jigsaw puzzle, the Lego set and the teacups. I went straight for my favorite treasure at the bottom.

Violet spotted it as I tugged it free. She gasped.

Victory. Sweet, sweet victory.

"HELLO? ANYONE IN HERE?" Maddox called as his knuckles rapped on the doorway to Violet's room.

I glanced up from the book we were reading as Maddox flipped open the flap of our tent and bent to look inside.

"Hey, Daddy." Violet smiled. "We built a tent."

"Hey, beautiful. It looks great."

"We'd better get started cleaning it up." I closed the book and set it aside. Then nudged Violet. "Ready?"

She nodded and crawled out first.

I collected the other books we'd been reading, or having Violet read to me for practice, then joined her and Maddox outside the tent.

"Are you done working?" Violet asked him.

He nodded, his gaze skeptical as he looked between the two of us. "Uh . . . yeah. I'm done."

"Can we do something fun?"

"Sure." He kept looking between us, the crease between his eyebrows deepening. Even I was a little shocked at how quickly Violet's attitude had changed.

I'd won our war using the oldest trick in the book.

Good, old-fashioned bribery.

"Let's clean up first," I told Violet. "Then I'll get out of here."

"Okay." She immediately went to work, dismantling the blankets we'd hauled out of the closet.

Hannah had come in mid-construction and given us extra sheets. That had been after a delightful lunch of grilled cheese and tomato bisque made by the chef.

As Violet and I had sat at the dining room table, eating in comfortable silence, both Hannah and Keith had joined us. Not long after, Heath and Tobias had arrived for a meal. The only Holiday missing had been Maddox.

The looks of sheer amazement at Violet's behavior had been a balm to my soul.

Had I worked a Holiday miracle? *Yes. Yes, I had.*

The satisfaction of taming Violet was nearly worth as much as I was being paid for this job.

Maddox joined to help tear apart the tent, folding a blanket beside me. He leaned in close to whisper, "There are no missing limbs. And no blood. I was expecting blood."

I grinned and picked up one of the pillows we'd been using as our tent floor. "Not today."

Assembling the tent had taken an hour. Dismantling less than ten minutes.

When it was done, Maddox bent to kiss his daughter's hair. "How was your day?"

"Fun." She looked up to me, and I gave her a wink. "Can we go in the hot tub?"

"Yes, but not until after dinner."

Violet frowned. "But—"

I cleared my throat and that frown disappeared.

She shot me a look, then muttered, "Okay."

Maddox's mouth fell open.

"Thanks for a fun day, Violet. I'll see you after Christmas."

"With your bag."

I nodded. "With my bag."

"Okay, good. Daddy, can I have some screen time?"

"Go ahead. Your iPad is in the theater room."

Violet raced away without a backward glance.

"What did you do with my real daughter and can we keep the imposter for the night?"

I laughed and walked to the bed to pick up my bag. With it slung over my shoulder, I patted its side. "Bribery works nine out of ten times."

"What's in there?"

"I'll never tell." I zipped my lips shut, then headed for the door.

"You're really not going to tell me?" Maddox asked, catching up to me in the hallway.

"Nope." I smirked. "That's between Violet and me."

"Today seemed to go better."

"Second days usually do. She's a good kid. The feisty ones are always the most fun."

Maddox stopped, his jaw slackened.

"What?" I slowed.

He swallowed hard. "You're the first nanny to ever tell

THE NAUGHTY, THE NICE AND THE NANNY

me she was a good kid."

"Seriously?" My heart squeezed. That was, well . . . awful.

"Seriously." He pressed a hand to his heart and the smile he gave me was blinding.

"Oh." A blush crept into my cheeks. "Well, she is. But can I give you some unsolicited advice? You can say no."

"Please."

I didn't want to overstep, but today had been surprisingly easy. Wrangling Violet hadn't been the challenge I'd expected. Yes, I'd bribed her all morning, but along with each reward had come some firm and unwavering rules. She'd followed them without fail. Not only was she spirited, but that girl was incredibly smart.

"She has so much potential. She's funny and witty and thoughtful. She notices more than most kids her age. And she has these sweet moments when she just melts your heart."

Maddox beamed under his daughter's praise.

"But . . ."

Off went the light.

"She wants attention. She needs boundaries. And she's maybe a little . . . spoiled."

He raked a hand through his hair. "That's my fault. I don't spend enough time with her, and so during the time we do have, I can't seem to tell her no."

"I get it. I've worked for a lot of parents with demanding careers."

"What did they do?"

"Hired me, of course," I teased. "I don't have the answer. One of the moms I worked for would cook dinner with her kids every Friday night. Another family had game night on Tuesdays. It doesn't have to be all day, every day. Just something special that you stick to. Find out what works for you and Violet."

"I will." He nodded. "Thanks. For today and for the advice."

We walked down the hallway toward the staircase. As soon as we reached the balcony, the scent of fresh pine from the Christmas tree filled my nose. Mixed with Maddox's spicy cologne, the combination was intoxicating. My fingers glided over the smooth handrail, and for just a moment, I let myself pretend that he remembered me.

"I was hoping to ask you for a favor," Maddox said as he escorted me to the door.

"What favor?" I plucked my coat from a hook and pulled it on. Unless he asked me to give up sugar in December, whatever favor he asked for—sexual or not—would likely be met with a resounding yes.

"Tomorrow night is my family's annual Christmas party downtown. Mom and Dad invite a ton of their friends. They normally host it the week before Christmas, but the place was booked for a wedding, so the timing worked out that this year it falls on Christmas Eve. I guess enough of their friends didn't mind so they went ahead and scheduled it. I haven't been home for the party in years, but it means a lot to them. And I'd really like it to go off without a hitch."

"You need someone to watch Violet."

"Please." Oh, God, he was giving me the *save-me-Natalie* eyes. How was I supposed to say no to that look?

"I know you're under no obligation to help, but I don't know anyone else. There will be a lot of people who want my attention at the party, and I heard you a few minutes ago. Violet needs my attention too. But this party . . . I'll be swarmed. Everyone will want to know about why I'm moving home and what I'll be doing with my business. I don't want Violet to have to hang by my side, bored to tears the whole time. She's never been to this party either and I'd like her to have a good time. And, uh . . . there was an incident."

"Uh-oh."

"Full disclosure. Last year, I took Violet to a New Year's Eve party in LA. It was the same situation. I was bombarded and she snuck away to the kitchen. She pulled over an entire rack filled with three hundred crème brûlées."

"Eek."

"Ask me if we were invited back this year."

I giggled. "Your kid has style, I'll give her that."

"Just a few hours."

Christmas Eve was my least favorite non-holiday, holiday. Usually I'd spend time with my family, but Christmas Eve typically involved a last-minute trip to the mall and

I'd spend hours being bumped into by husbands who'd forgotten to buy their wives gifts.

So many people loved the anticipation that came with Christmas Eve. Me? Not so much.

I was patient in many ways, but when it came to gifts and orgasms, I preferred instant gratification.

As tempting as Dad's famous Cheez Whiz charcuterie board was not, a fancy downtown soiree might make Christmas Eve bearable. I'd heard about the Holiday Christmas party for years but had never been invited. And this year, Maddox Holiday himself was asking me to attend.

Yeah, it was as the hired help but fourteen-year-old me didn't give a crap about that detail.

For her, this would practically be a prom date.

"Do I get to wear a fancy dress?"

"If that makes you happy, then yes. If that makes you lean toward a no, then wear pajamas and slippers."

"I like fancy dresses." It wasn't uncommon for clients to ask me to attend special events. I happened to have a few dresses that I'd bought for those rare occasions and each was collecting dust in my closet.

The corner of his mouth turned up. "Seven o'clock. The Baxter."

"I'll see you there." I reached for the doorknob, but Maddox beat me to it, brushing my knuckles with his fingertips. Sparks flew beneath my skin. The air crackled between us.

He stilled, his eyes finding mine. Then they dropped, tracing the line of my nose before landing on my mouth. His Adam's apple bobbed.

We stood there, too close for a moment too long, until he cleared his throat, and I pulled my hand away, ducking my chin to hide my smile.

Maddox Holiday had just stared at my lips, and unless my radar was broken—it might be—he'd felt the sparks too.

Teenage Natalie did a fist pump.

Adult Natalie smacked teenage Natalie's hand.

You're his employee. Sort-of employee. There were boundaries I wouldn't cross. Not again.

The cool air from outside was welcome on my over-heated cheeks as he opened the door. I expected him to wave from the porch, but instead he fell into step beside me as we walked to my car. He even opened the back door for me to stow my bag.

"See you tomorrow, Nat. Everyone used to call you Nat, right?"

"They did. Your mom said you guys went through old yearbooks last night. Did your brothers tell you that?"

"No." He tapped his temple and smiled that sexy smile. His dimple appeared and my heart did a cartwheel in the snow. "Tomorrow."

Tomorrow.

One word and I was already starting to like this Christmas Eve.

CHAPTER FOUR

MADDOX

"Which tie, princess?" I held up a black one and a red one.

Violet immediately pointed to the red—no surprise.

"Red it is." I laid it on my bed beside the suit she'd picked out, then checked the clock. I needed to get in the shower but I wanted to make sure Violet was ready for tonight first. "Let's do your hair. Then I'll get ready too."

"Are there going to be any other kids there tonight?" she asked as I steered her down the hallway toward her bedroom.

"I think so. And Natalie will be there with us. Nana and Papa. Uncle Heath and Uncle Tobias. It's usually a lot of fun."

"Can I stay up late?"

"Definitely. And you can have extra dessert."

"Yessss." She clapped and skipped ahead to her room.

She was wearing a red dress with roses on the wide collar. The front hem was cut higher than the back, and she'd chosen her gold glitter shoes in place of her favorite red.

She looked beautiful.

She looked grown up.

While I'd been working my ass off, my daughter had become this young person. This incredible, smart young person. No longer a baby. No longer a toddler. She was simply . . . my Violet.

We'd spent the day together today and the realization that I'd missed out on too much had hit me like a freight train. A change was overdue.

When I reached the bathroom, I found her standing by the vanity, running a brush through her hair. She didn't need me to comb out the strands anymore. She didn't need me to prop her on the counter so she could see in the mirror. She didn't need me to help her brush her teeth.

I choked on the lump in my throat that had been there since breakfast. "I had fun with you today."

"Me too." She smiled. I'd seen more of those smiles in the past twelve hours than I'd seen in twelve months.

Natalie had been right. Violet needed my attention, and I needed, well . . . Violet.

My daughter wasn't the only one who'd smiled more today.

We'd gone out to breakfast at a diner on Main. We'd ventured to a few shops, braving the Christmas Eve crowds to shop for some last-minute gifts. Then we'd spent the rest of the day doing whatever Violet had wanted.

She'd showed me some of her favorite YouTube videos on the iPad. We'd devoured a dozen Christmas cookies—next week I'd have to add thirty minutes to my daily work-outs to burn them off. We'd played checkers. We'd started a jigsaw puzzle. We'd hit the hot tub and played pool in the game room.

"What are we doing with your hair?" I took the brush from her hand and ran it through her tresses.

Cece had always done Violet's hair. She'd also picked out our daughter's clothes. Violet's appearance was the one thing that Cece had seemed interested in when it came to our child. It was the reason Violet loved red so much. Cece had always found Violet red clothes. Even now, the rare gifts she'd send were typically red. Though the last two dresses had been in the wrong size.

But Violet hadn't cared that they'd been too small. And every time I brought home an outfit in blue or green or pink, I'd earn a scowl and a glare.

Fucking Cece.

She hadn't called once in the past week. I doubted she remembered that tomorrow was Christmas. There'd be no gift for Violet waiting under the tree from her mother.

For the past couple of years, I'd wrapped a present and had labeled it from Cece. I'd made sure the paper and bow were different than anything my assistant had put on the gifts I'd bought.

This year . . . I hadn't had the energy.

I wasn't going to keep pretending that Cece gave a shit, because in the end, I was only delaying the inevitable. Sooner than later, Violet would realize that her mother wasn't interested in her life. I could probably put it off for a few more years, but the hurt was coming, one way or another.

Now that we were moving to Montana, it was time to stop pretending.

Cece wasn't here to do Violet's hair. But I was. And damn it, I'd do everything in my power to be enough.

"I could dig the curling iron out of the suitcases," I said.

Violet's eyes widened in the mirror.

"Okay, no curling iron." The last time I'd tried, there'd been a near-burn incident. "How about a twist?"

In the past couple of years, I'd watched countless videos on how to do braids and twists. While curling-iron skills evaded me, I could wield a bobby pin like a pro.

"Nana bought me a tiara. Can I wear it with a twist?" she asked.

"Sure."

Off she raced into her bedroom, coming back moments later with a smile as bright as the crystals on the tiara. I got to work with the pins, taking strands of her thick, dark hair —my hair—and twisting them up onto the crown of her head. Then when all of the pieces were secure, I placed the tiara.

"Well?"

She turned her face, looking at both sides, then gave me the nod of approval. "I like it."

"Good." If that hairdo lasted all night, I'd be shocked. "So before we go to the party, I have a question for you."

"What?"

"Will you make me a deal?"

"What kind of deal?"

I picked her up and set her on the bathroom counter. "No trouble tonight. This is something Nana and Papa do every year and it means a lot to them. Please be good and listen to Natalie."

"Okay," she muttered.

"Thank you." I kissed her forehead.

"Is Natalie going to be my new nanny when we move here?"

"No." Though I'd already contemplated asking the agency if she was available. Violet had dropped her name a few times today as we'd played, which had never happened with another nanny. Violet seemed to forget them the minute they walked out the door. "She's just hanging out with us for Christmas."

"Oh." She dropped her gaze to her lap.

"Do you want her to be your new nanny?"

Violet shrugged.

That shrug was the equivalent to a five-star review. Natalie had clearly made an impression. On us both.

She'd been on my mind nearly all day. The softness in

her blue eyes. The sweet smile. Her musical laugh. Foolish as it was, I couldn't wait to see her tonight.

"Daddy?" Violet peeked up at me from beneath her lashes.

"Violet."

"Is Mommy moving here with us?"

Hell. I hated Cece for making me answer this question. "No, honey. She's not moving here. It will just be us."

"Hmm." She looked to the brush on the countertop, staring at her own hairs stuck in its teeth.

"Do you like it here?" In all the months I'd been planning this, I hadn't asked my daughter if she enjoyed Montana. Here she was, screaming for attention, and I was so busy planning a relocation that I hadn't noticed.

"It's okay."

"We'll be closer to Nana and Papa."

She nodded. "I like their hot tub."

"What if we didn't have a nanny when we moved here? What if we had more days like today?"

Her eyes flew to mine and the hope in them nearly broke my heart. "Really?"

"You might have to have babysitters if I get super busy. And you might have to spend some days with Nana and Papa because they get lonely for you. But most days, it will just be me and you. What do you think?"

"Do I have to go to school?"

I chuckled. "Yes, you have to go to school."

"I don't have any friends here."

"I know." I touched a fingertip to her nose. "But you'll make new friends. Great friends."

"Maddox?" My mother's voice carried from the hallway.

"In here, Mom." I lifted Violet off the counter, then we headed out to meet my mom.

"Oh, look at you." Mom clutched her hands to her heart when she saw Violet. "You look beautiful, darling."

"Thanks, Nana." Violet beamed and touched her tiara.

"You look gorgeous, Mom." I leaned in to kiss her cheek. She was wearing a pretty green dress with a matching jacket, embroidered with a shimmery thread of the same color. Her hair was pinned back, much like Violet's, and her makeup flawless.

"Thank you." Mom cupped my cheek, then she realized I was wearing jeans and a long-sleeved T-shirt. "You're not dressed. Why are you not dressed? We're leaving in thirty minutes."

"Don't worry, I'll be ready." I winked at Violet, then left her with Mom while I rushed to my bathroom for a quick shower and a shave. Dressed in my black suit, I knotted my tie and made it downstairs with five minutes to spare.

"We'll drive separately," I told Mom and Dad.

"See you there." Dad nodded and headed for the garage. Violet and I were close behind him, going to the Audi SUV I'd rented for this trip.

"Wait for me." Heath appeared in the doorway, a beer

in hand. He dropped the bottle in the trash can, then rounded the Audi's hood for the passenger side. "You're my DD tonight."

"What's a DD?" Violet asked from her booster seat in the back.

"Something I'll teach you about when you're older," I answered.

Heath twisted in his seat, giving Violet a grin and fist bump. "Excited for tonight?"

"Yes," she answered.

"How about you, brother?"

"I am." This was the first time in years I was truly looking forward to a party. My family was one reason. Natalie was another.

"Heard you took a day off," Heath said. "How'd that treat you?"

"Not bad. Thinking of making a habit of it."

"Yeah?"

"It's time. And someone told me about this new thing. They call it vacation."

He chuckled. "Good advice. I bet that someone is ridiculously smart. And handsome. And hung like a—"

I smacked his shoulder. "Young ears."

"Sorry. In all seriousness. Are you really going to step back?"

"Yeah. I am." I'd made billions of dollars in my short career. My team was talented and capable, but even if the wheels came off the bus, if it crashed and burned, it didn't really matter.

My financial future was locked in. So was Violet's.

"I can't keep working like this," I confessed, glancing to the rearview mirror. "It's not fair to her."

"Listen, I think it's great you're coming home. We've all missed you these past seven years, especially Mom and Dad. They think *you know who* is Satan's mistress for trapping you in California."

"They're not wrong," I muttered.

While we'd been married, Cece hadn't enjoyed visiting Bozeman. Even after the divorce, my infrequent visits to Montana hadn't been enough, and with Mom and Dad's busy careers, it was hard for them to get to LA more than two or three times a year.

"But . . ." Heath said, his tone growing serious. "Before you come up here, I need to ask you an important question."

"Okay," I drawled.

"Can you get me early access to the last season of *State of Ruin?*"

I chuckled. "It's really good. I watched the final episode on the flight here."

"I need it." Heath groaned. "Please? I have not once played the brother card. But I'm calling it in."

"Consider it your Christmas present. But don't tell anyone."

"Yes." He grinned. "I'm binging tomorrow unless I'm too hungover to function."

My company, Madcast, produced and distributed *State of Ruin*. We were the fastest growing streaming video service in the world.

My lucky break had come my senior year in college when I'd been out at a bar, drinking at some run down joint and bullshitting with the guy on a stool beside mine. He'd turned out to be one of the most famous directors in Hollywood.

He'd told me about a screenplay that he'd drafted, but no matter who he'd pitched it to, the major media companies weren't buying. They'd wanted him as a director, not a writer, but screenwriting had been his passion.

When I'd gotten a full-ride academic scholarship to UCLA, Mom and Dad had gifted me my college tuition. Responsible kid that I'd been, I'd saved most of it.

A magazine reporter who'd interviewed me a few years ago had written that it had been divine intervention that I hadn't spent that money. Because instead of blowing it on a car and spring-break vacations, I'd used it to buy that screenplay and the rights to the show. I'd also partnered with the director to make a low-budget version of season one.

It had gone viral and been picked up by one of my current competitors. They'd done well on it. The director and I had both made money from the sale. He'd gone on to other projects while I'd taken that money and used it as the seed for Madcast.

Fast-forward seven years from that conversation in the bar, and we'd had countless hits in all the major genres—drama, documentaries, comedy, children, romance. *State of Ruin*, a worldwide phenomenon, was poised to be our biggest show yet. If you wanted the best of the best film and television entertainment, you paid Madcast eleven ninety-nine a month for a subscription.

We'd become a publicly traded company three years ago and our stock price was at its highest value yet. I was the majority shareholder and CEO.

Some people said I had a gift for choosing projects. Mostly, I selected the ones that sounded like something I'd watch. I'd read books and buy the film rights because even though I loved TV, books were almost always better. That, and there was an endless supply of incredible stories waiting for the screen. My team helped fill in the gaps as they had damn good taste too.

Moving away from California was a risk. I'd miss the day-to-day happenings at headquarters, but I'd regret missing Violet's life even more. If the board had a problem with me in this new satellite office, I'd step down as CEO and let someone else run the show.

There were countless opportunities for a man with my wealth. Leaving Madcast would be hard as hell, but I'd start something new in Bozeman if I had to.

"So, Violet." Heath twisted in his seat to talk over his

shoulder. "Nana told me that Natalie brought you a bag of secrets yesterday. Want to tell me what was in the bag?"

"No." She stared out her window.

"Come on. Tell me," Heath begged.

She zipped her lips closed, just like Natalie had done.

"It's no use." I laughed at Heath's frown. Whatever Natalie had done to get Violet's silence and loyalty had been ironclad. "Trust me. I asked her no less than fifty times today and she's not talking."

"Natalie's a magician," Heath said, dropping his voice.

"You're not wrong."

He rubbed his hands together as we approached Main Street. "I love this party."

Glittering garlands were strung over the street. Trees glowed with their strings of white lights. Stores were decked out for the season. There was truly nothing like a Christmas in Bozeman. With any luck, we wouldn't be missing any more.

"I wonder who will cause the drama this year," Heath said.

"Maybe there won't be drama."

"There'd better be." He scoffed. "That's the best part of the party."

I shook my head, smiling, and pulled into a parking lot. Then we all piled out and, with Violet's hand in mine, headed toward the hotel.

"Excited?" I asked her.

She nodded, her eyes wide and full of wonder as she

took it all in. As we walked through the hotel's gold and glass doors, she squeezed my hand tighter.

The lobby of The Baxter was bustling with people, some going into the adjoining restaurants. Others stood at the small bar, laughing and talking with a festive cocktail in their hands.

I shrugged off my coat and helped Violet out of hers. With them draped over my arm, I stood straight, ready to head upstairs where the party was held. But when I looked up, the sight that greeted me sent my jaw to the marble floor.

Natalie was descending the grand staircase that led to the second-floor ballroom.

She was definitely not in pajamas. Her strappy heels sank into the plush maroon carpet covering each step. Her decadent body was wrapped in a fitted black gown that hugged her slight curves. A slit ran up the gown's side, showcasing one toned leg with miles of smooth skin.

Other than that slit, the dress was simple, with long sleeves and a high neckline. On any other woman, it would have been demure.

On Natalie, it was pure sin.

My mouth went dry.

It had been a long, long time since the mere sight of a woman rendered me speechless.

"I should have paid more attention to Nat in school," Heath whispered at my side, his eyes locked on her bare thigh. He took one step, ready to pounce, but my hand shot out and grabbed his elbow.

"Don't even think about it. She's mine." The claim blurted from my mouth before my brain could engage.

A slow grin spread across his face. "Gotcha. I wondered if you might have a thing for her."

"There's no thing." *Shit.* "She's . . . my nanny."

"Right. Whatever you say, brother." He'd heard the possession in my voice. The claim. Backtracking was pointless.

"Good luck." Heath clapped me on the shoulder, then jogged up the stairs, giving Natalie a smile and nod as he passed.

She reached the bottom step and walked toward us. It took considerable effort not to drool over the silhouette of her body and that damn leg that peeked through with every other one of her graceful strides.

The blood rushed to my cock and I shifted, holding the coats over my groin in an attempt to hide the growing bulge behind my pants. *Christ.*

She was the nanny. This was a business relationship only, and for my daughter's sake, one I couldn't afford to fuck up.

The moment we got up the stairs, I'd let her take Violet and I'd get a strong drink. Just one so I could drive us home later. Or fuck it, maybe I'd get smashed and we'd catch a ride with my parents.

Natalie smiled as she came closer, which only made my arousal grow.

Drunk. Definitely drunk. Maybe that would help me control this urge to sink my lips onto hers.

"Hello." She waved at me, then gave her undivided attention to my daughter. "You look beautiful, Violet."

"Thanks." Violet did a half twirl, twisting so her skirt would sway. She looked up to me and nodded toward the enormous tree in the corner and the bowl of candy canes being pilfered by the other kids in the lobby. "Can I go look at the tree?"

"Sure. Come right back."

Violet nodded, then darted away.

Natalie stood and took me in. Her gaze stopped on my throat, like she could see my heart stuck there.

When her hand came out to straighten the knot on my tie, I lost the battle with my will. "You look magnificent."

"Thank you." Her cheeks flushed. "It's fun to get dressed up."

"Fun is not the word I'd use for that dress." Sexy. Stunning. Maybe fun if I was the man stripping it from her body.

Natalie tucked a lock of hair behind her ear, pulling her lips in to hide a smile. "You're looking pretty sharp yourself, Mr. Holiday."

Mr. Holiday. My last name had never sounded so good. "Maddox."

"Maddox."

THE NAUGHTY, THE NICE AND THE NANNY

God, this woman. How had she not called me by my name? Now I wanted to hear her say it over and over, preferably while she was naked in my bed.

Fuck my life. I'd just broken my own damn rule. Never in my life had I flirted with a nanny. There'd never been a desire. But Natalie didn't fit the typical mold.

She was sassy. Smart. Sexy. And she liked my kid.

Maybe I should have felt guilty for this attraction.

I didn't.

Instead, I waited for Violet to come back from the tree, then offered Natalie my arm. "Shall we?"

CHAPTER FIVE

NATALIE

This was so surreal. It wasn't a date. *It's not a date.* The hours spent repeating that sentence while getting dressed up for the party had worked. When I'd showed up at The Baxter, I'd been ready for an evening shift with Violet.

But then Maddox had strolled through the doors with that confident, sexy swagger. One glance at him in that tailored suit and I'd skyrocketed to fantasyland. The man was so hot he could turn the lobby's Christmas tree into kindling with a single sultry look.

This was not a date.

But what if it was? I was giving myself the climb to the second floor to pretend.

The heat from his arm radiated through his jacket as we ascended the staircase. Never in my life had I thought I'd be walking into a party on Maddox's arm.

With every step, I felt the pressure of eyes aimed our way. Maddox was a billionaire, and even though he didn't live in Bozeman, his success made him a local celebrity in his small hometown.

A quick glance over my shoulder and I saw more than one gaze aimed at his face. To be fair, it was a fantastic face. We reached the ballroom and the conversation inside it died. For a split second, the only sound was the holiday-themed background music.

Maddox commanded attention and all eyes swung his way.

My way.

"Daddy, there's punch." Violet let go of his hand to point to a table with various carafes and pitchers. She was totally unfazed by the people staring. Then again, she was part of Maddox's orbit and probably used to the spotlight. "Can I get a drink?"

"Sure. You need to stay in this ballroom or with Natalie. All night, got it?"

"Got it." Then she was gone, her dress a red streak across the space.

"Thanks for the escort." I slid my arm free of his.

"My pleasure." Maddox grinned as he looked down. His blue eyes sparkled. They were almost . . . flirty?

No. No way. Maybe?

Filling my lungs was a challenge. My imagination had hitched a ride on Santa's sleigh and was soaring to new levels. Just the notion that Maddox might find me attractive was insane.

The crowd came to my rescue, bringing my feet to earth. As Maddox had suspected, people began moving our way. In moments, he'd be inundated.

"I'd better catch up with Violet."

"Save me a dance later?"

"Um . . ." What. The. Christmas Fudge. "Sure?"

His grin widened, then he was swallowed up by guests. He stood taller than most until Keith came over to shake his hand.

I tore my eyes away and spotted Violet. In both hands, she clutched a plastic cup nearly overflowing with cherry liquid. At least if she spilled, it would blend with her dress.

She put it to her lips and the smile she gave after the first swallow was so sweet, I found myself smiling too.

"Nat!" A wave caught the corner of my eye and some of the nerves from the party vanished at seeing a familiar face coming my way.

I waved back and crossed the room. "Hey, Stella."

"It's so good to see you." She pulled me into a hug.

Stella and I had been friends since high school. She'd been a freshman on the swim team my junior year. No sweeter soul had ever graced the pool. All these years later and we'd stayed in touch, meeting for a drink now and then to catch up. I'd tell her about the kids I was watching, and she'd entertain me with her older brother's latest antics.

"I had no idea you'd be here," she said.

"It was a last-minute invite. I'm actually here to work."

At that moment, Violet appeared at my side, her punch cup empty. "Can I have more?"

I laughed. "Let's pace ourselves. We have all night."

"How are you?" Stella asked. "It's been forever."

Before I could answer, Heath appeared at her side along with Stella's brother.

Guy was midsentence when he noticed me and did a double take. "Natalie?"

"Hey. Good to see you, Guy."

"Been a while."

We'd graduated together but it had been a while since we'd bumped into one another. Guy had always been a source of entertainment. He'd been our class clown. The boy who'd try anything, no matter how reckless. Wherever Heath and Tobias had gone, Guy had been close to follow. Our lockers had been beside each other's, and he'd always had an extra piece of his spearmint gum to share.

He was chewing some tonight, his jaw working as he checked out my ass.

"Guy." I waited until he looked at my face, then I gave him a headshake.

"You sure?"

I giggled. "Quite. But thanks anyway."

He chuckled. "Are you here alone?"

"Nope." I looked down to Violet, holding out my hand to take hers. "Violet's my date tonight. And we're raiding the dessert table before any of the good stuff disappears."

"Natalie's the coolest of the cool," Stella told her. "You're going to have a blast tonight."

"But not as cool as Uncle Heath, right?" Heath held out his hand for Violet to smack it.

She ignored him.

"Ouch." Heath feigned a wound to the heart.

Stella laughed, a blush coloring her cheeks as she looked to him. She'd had a tiny crush on him in high school. Clearly it hadn't gone away.

Heath glanced at her, his gaze drifting down the low-cut V of her dress. He tore his eyes away, too quickly, when Guy nudged his arm and jerked his chin to the door.

A cute brunette and a petite blonde had just walked into the ballroom.

"Be my wingman," Guy said. "Hit on the blonde."

"Um . . ." Heath rubbed the back of his neck, looking to Stella.

She was studying her heels.

Guy clapped Heath on the shoulder, steering him away and leaving Stella crestfallen.

"You okay?" I bumped elbows with Stella.

"Great!" She winced at her own volume.

"I didn't know you'd be here tonight."

"I just started working at Holiday Homes." She shrugged. "Keith invites the whole office. I was actually going to skip and go to church with my parents, then hang out at home, but Guy talked me into coming. He promised to hang out with me because his girlfriend just dumped him. He's kind of broken up about it, even though he won't admit it. I felt bad for him, so I told him I'd be his date. But . . . he just ditched me."

"Want to hang with us?"

"I think I'm going to grab a drink." She smiled at us both, then nodded toward the bar.

The bar where Heath was now standing alone. Sans the blonde. I guess he'd already shirked his wingman duties.

"Have fun." I winked, then tugged on Violet's hand. "Sugar time?"

"How many desserts can I have before dinner?"

"One."

"Four," she countered.

"One."

"Three."

I arched an eyebrow. "One."

Her eye roll was spectacular. By the time she hit sixteen, she'd be able to teach a masterclass on attitude. "Fine. One."

"Glad we could agree."

She got two, which I blamed on her father. While we were at the dessert table, eyeing the assortments of mini cakes and cookies and candies, I'd caught sight of Maddox.

From across the room I'd felt his pull. His allure.

He'd been surrounded by men, all wearing suits and ties with cocktails in their grips. Each one of them hanging on Maddox's every word. When he spoke, you listened to that deep, soothing voice. I'd been too far away to hear whatever it was he'd been saying, yet still, I'd been glued to the sight of his mouth moving, his lips forming words.

Violet had snuck a second cookie while I'd been drooling over the way he'd combed his hair tonight. Dark and stylish, pulled artfully away from a part over his left eyebrow. He'd kept one hand in his pocket while the other had held a tumbler with a gin and tonic. Whenever he'd smiled, that sexy dimple would pop on his clean-shaven face.

Violet reached for a caramel, thinking I wasn't watching, but I caught her fingers. "Let's get away from this table."

The band's lead singer took the microphone and welcomed the growing crowd. As the caterers swept into the room carrying trays of heavy hors d'oeuvres, he crooned the beginning of a sultry jazz number that enticed couples to the dance floor.

The space was a simple square with a row of windows on the exterior walls to overlook Main Street. Cocktail tables had been staged with white tablecloths. The ballroom's crystal chandelier cast a golden glow over the guests. The bar in the corner would be a popular spot.

"What do you think of the party?" I asked Violet as we lapped the room.

"It's nice. Some of the parties Daddy took me to at home are way bigger though. But they were *so* boring."

"Every single one? Come on. I bet one of them was fun, wasn't it?"

"Well, this one time, we got to go to a pool party. There was a waterslide and noodles and a lot of other kids to play with."

"Oooh. Now you're talking. I love pool parties and swimming is my favorite thing ever."

"Really?"

I nodded. "We have a couple of days together after Christmas. Maybe I'll see if I can convince your dad to let me take you swimming. What do you say?"

"Yessss." Her smile widened, then dropped in a flash. "Daddy didn't pack my floaties. They're still at home. I can stand up in Nana and Papa's hot tub but he doesn't let me swim in a pool without my floaties."

"Don't worry. I won't let you sink. I teach kids how to swim."

"You do?" She cocked her head to the side, staring at me like I was this entirely different person.

"Yes." I giggled. "Want me to teach you how to swim?"

"Okay." She nodded so wildly that her tiara came loose.

I fixed her crown, then we wandered around the ballroom, stopping at every window to peer outside. We ate food, hunting down different trays when something caught our eye. We refilled our punch cups twice. And when she got bored watching the adults, we escaped the ballroom and ventured downstairs for a change of scenery and closer inspection of the tree.

Once I found a topic Violet liked, she became this animated, wonderful storyteller. From her favorite books to cartoons to games, she was pure entertainment. Minute by minute, she was letting her guard down.

The party was in full swing by the time we returned to the second floor, the noise having doubled.

Keith spotted us as we walked through the doors and his whole face lit up when he looked at his granddaughter. "Violet, there you are. I was hoping you'd be my first dance. Wanna boogie?"

"A boogie? Eww." She giggled and took his hand, letting him lead her to the floor.

I hovered by the wall, watching as he twirled her around and made her laugh. She really was a beautiful child, inside and out. She was shy at times. Incredibly sweet at others, like how there'd only been one double chocolate cookie left, and when we'd both reached for it, she'd insisted I take it. The more she talked, the more her personality came alive. Her spirit was enchanting.

The naughty girl I'd met just days ago was nowhere in sight, which only confirmed my suspicions. That attitude of hers was an act to attract Maddox's attention. That, or her mother's. Not that Violet had mentioned her mom, not even once.

"So this is where you've been hiding." Maddox's

rugged voice snapped me out of my trance. He stepped beside me, his suit jacket brushing against the sleeve of my dress. "Dance with me."

God, it was sexy that he didn't ask. "Don't feel obligated to entertain me. I'm fine."

"Actually, you're the only one in the room who I *want* to talk to. So I thought maybe you could entertain me." He held out his hand and maybe a different woman would have had the power to resist, but the moment my palm slid against his, any notion of objecting vanished.

Wide and warm with long fingers, his hand enveloped mine as he whisked me to the dance floor and swept me into his arms, holding me closer than was professional.

The scent of his spicy cologne filled my nose. The strength of his arm banded around my hip. The temptation of those lips was heady. Fuck professionalism. This was my only chance to dance with Maddox Holiday.

My prom dreams were coming true.

"I'm not a great dancer," he confessed as his fingertips pressed in deeper to the small of my back.

"Oh, I'd say you're doing fine." I followed his lead, savoring the feel of his body pressed to mine.

"Having fun tonight?"

I nodded. "I am."

"How is Violet doing?"

"Good. She is wholly entertaining. And I mean that as a compliment."

He chuckled and turned us, both searching out his

daughter. She was still dancing with Keith. "Thanks for hanging with her."

"You are paying me."

"This is true. I can still say thank you."

Boy, he was something. Genuine. Nice. Sexy. My cheeks flushed and I dropped my gaze to his sinful red tie. Visions of undoing that Windsor knot and flipping the buttons free on his starched white shirt flooded my mind and I glanced at the couples around us, looking anywhere but at Maddox.

"Are you having fun?" I asked, trying to put a little space between us. Anything to ease the bloom of desire spreading in my lower belly.

Maddox wouldn't have it. He pulled me closer, flush against his hard planes. "I am now."

Oh, sweet baby Jesus in the manger. "Are you flirting with me?"

"I am. Do you mind?"

"No," I confessed, looking up to meet his gaze. What single woman in her right mind would object to Maddox Holiday flirting with her?

"Excellent." He spun us in a circle, the smile on his face widening. "But to answer your question, it's been . . . what I expected. I think I've told every business associate of Dad's in attendance that yes, business is good. Yes, I'm moving here at some point. And no, I'm not interested in investing in their next great idea. For the rest of the night,

I'm ignoring anyone in a suit unless they have the last name Holiday."

"Good thing I'm in a dress."

He chuckled. "And a very nice dress it is."

"There you go, flirting with me again."

"I haven't flirted with anyone in a long, long time. I forgot how much fun it could be."

"Who's the last woman you flirted with?"

His smile faded a bit. "My ex-wife."

"Ah." Whoops. "Sorry."

"Don't be."

"So . . ." Time to change the subject. "You should know that I promised Violet I'd teach her how to swim. I hope you don't mind."

"Fine by me." His grip on my hand tightened as we moved the other direction. The song had changed but we'd just kept on dancing. "I should have gotten her into private lessons ages ago. We've got a pool at our place in LA and she loves to swim. She's got the basics and safety techniques down, but I guess I'm paranoid and overprotective. I don't let her swim without water wings unless I'm in the pool with her."

"I promise I'm qualified. And if she's comfortable in the water, it won't take her long to feel confident."

"I trust you."

Those words warmed my heart.

"What was in the bag?" he asked. "Your magic tote."

"Violet didn't tell you?"

He shook his head. "No."

"Good for her." A lot of children would have spilled our secret. "It was a family-sized bag of M&M's. Swedish Fish. Skittles. I had toys and games too, but I decided to go straight for the candy."

"I should have guessed." He laughed. "She's got a mouth full of sweet teeth. That was part of the reason for the crème brûlée fiasco at that party last year. When I asked her why she'd climbed up that rack, she told me it was because she wanted the biggest one and they probably kept the big ones on top."

"I believe it." I laughed. "When I pulled that bag of M&M's out and started eating them, her entire attitude changed. It was just something to loosen her up. Something to bribe her with until she let down her guard and realized I wasn't her enemy."

"Smart."

I shrugged. "I've spent a lot of time with kids, working as a nanny and working with kids at the pool. They aren't all that complicated."

"What do you do with kids at the pool? Swimming lessons?"

"Sometimes. Mostly, I assist a physical therapist in town. He does pediatric aquatic therapy. That's what I want to do someday. Maybe. When I save enough to go to school and work up the courage to enroll. The idea of studying is . . ." I grimaced.

"You'd do great."

"Eeek. School? Granted, I always liked school but I haven't had to study in a long time. And I'm comfortable where I am."

"But it's not your dream."

I sighed. "No. It's not. I love kids but I have more to offer."

"Then it's time to step outside of your comfort zone."

Damn, but he was right. And motivating. One conversation and I was ready to dash to the admissions office at Montana State and hand them my application. If I wanted to become a physical therapist, I couldn't be a nanny forever. Maybe it was time to get serious.

Maddox let me go to twirl me beneath his arm, then hauled me back against his body, holding me close again.

"This is very surreal," I admitted.

"How so?"

"You're Maddox Holiday." *Duh.* "You had to know that every girl at Bozeman High was in love with you, including me."

Oh, hell. What was wrong with my mouth? Why couldn't it keep words on the inside?

The corner of his mouth turned up. "You were in love with me?"

"Maybe?" *Damn.* But now that it was out there, I might as well own it. "I was in love with you the way that awkward teenage girls love the smart, handsome boys who will never know they exist. Writing our names together in a heart. Naming our future children. Following you after class and home from school. Lurking outside your bedroom window, watching you sleep."

Maddox's feet ground to a halt.

I winked. "Kidding."

He threw his head back and laughed, a sound so warm and rich, it was worth whatever embarrassment from admitting my adolescent crush. He shook his head, the sparkle in his eye breathtaking as he smiled. "Well, you've got one thing wrong. I knew you existed."

"Did not."

"Did so. I saw you once at the pool, and I remember having to take a long, cold shower afterward."

I leaned back to study his face. "Seriously?"

"Swim caps. They get me every time."

I burst out laughing, relaxing as we moved together, dancing until the end of the song.

He kept my arm as he escorted me off the floor. "Should we join Violet at the dessert table?"

"Lead the way."

Violet stood beside Keith, each shoving cakes in their mouths. My watchful eye, even distracted by Maddox, hadn't strayed far from his daughter.

He'd had a pulse on her too. With every other turn, he'd searched for her. His love for her was written all over his face. And *my, my mistletoe* it was attractive.

"She's going to be up all night with the amount of sugar she's had," he said.

"Probably." I laughed. "I need to tell you something."

"What's that?"

I took in Violet as she plucked a cookie from a tray and handed it to Keith. I made out the words *the best ever* on her little lips before she took a cookie of her own. "You have a cool kid. She's almost impossible not to love."

Maddox stopped walking, forcing me to stop too. The expression on his face was almost . . . pained.

"What?" Had I said something wrong?

"You're killing me here."

"Why?"

He shook his head and let out a groan. "I have a policy. A firm policy. And I've never once wanted to break it until you."

"What policy?"

He leaned in close to whisper in my ear. The faint stubble from his cheek tickled mine as his breath caressed the shell of my ear. "Never kiss the nanny."

CHAPTER SIX

MADDOX

There was a very real chance that Natalie Buchanan was going to shatter my self-control.

Thirty-two nannies, and number thirty-three was going to be my ruin.

The scent of her hair wrapped around me, sweet like the most decadent dessert in the room. Her touch, warm and light, was the perfect caress on my arm. She was beautiful. Graceful. Enchanting.

But it was her intelligence and wit that would be my undoing. That, and her praise of my daughter.

No woman, besides my mother, had ever said they loved Violet. No other nannies. No friends. Not even Cece. I couldn't remember a time when I'd heard her tell Violet *I love you*.

But Natalie had said it—had meant it. After just days of knowing Violet.

I was putty in her delicate hands. One dance and I was in trouble.

"Sorry." I leaned away. "That was inappropriate."

Everything I'd done with her tonight had been inappropriate. The dancing. The flirting. Yet here I was, practically glued to her side.

"No apologies," she said, with a pretty flush in her cheeks. "The teenage girl inside me is doing backflips into the pool at the moment because of that comment. You just made her dreams come true."

"Glad I could help." I chuckled. Though it was time to remember that Nat wasn't my date, so I slipped my arm from hers and glanced around the room. "Who do you think it will be this year?"

"Who and what?"

"This party has become infamous. There's always someone who has too much to drink and gives the rest of us something to talk about for the year to come."

"Really? Everyone here seems so . . . snobby isn't the right word. Classy. Composed."

I laughed. "See the woman in the gray dress over by the tree in the corner?"

Natalie followed my gaze. "Yeah."

"The last time I was at this party, ages ago on a rare trip home from LA, she started stripping on the dance floor."

"Are you talking about the woman who looks like my

grandmother? Short gray hair. Pearl earrings. Probably in her early sixties."

"That's the one. She got all the way down to her slip before her husband realized what was happening and rushed over from the bar and took her home."

Natalie's eyes widened. "And she comes back here? I would have moved out of Bozeman by New Year's."

"I don't think she remembers and no one has the heart to tell her. That's sort of the unspoken rule at this party. What happens here, stays here."

"Ahh." She nodded. "Good to know."

"I missed it, but last year, Tobias told me that one of Dad's friends went around propositioning women to join him and his wife in a three-way. The wife didn't realize it was happening until he found a winner and introduced the two."

Natalie giggled. "I wonder how that conversation went."

"That's the three of them right there." I pointed to the trio at a cocktail table. Their heads were bent together, the women whispering a secret. The man kept eyeing them both, looking rather pleased with himself.

"Oh my God." Her eyes widened. "They totally hooked up, didn't they?"

"Definitely. Whatever keeps the magic alive, I guess. Though I'm not one for sharing, even if it is with another woman."

If I had Natalie in my bed, it would only be the two of us.

The flush in her cheeks deepened. "So, um . . . what else has happened?"

I spent the next ten minutes entertaining her with tales from past parties. I'd missed most of the embarrassing moments firsthand, but Tobias and Heath never failed to give me the play-by-play each year. And I knew my parents' friends well enough to place stories with faces. Some years hadn't been as exciting as others, but with Natalie's rapt attention and the smile on her face, I kept talking just because I didn't want her to walk away.

"I would not expect any of that from this crowd." Natalie laughed after my last story about the man who'd gotten drunk three years ago and convinced half the party to do tequila body shots.

"Every year. People let loose. Have a little fun."

"But body shots? A threesome? I'd expect that at a fraternity party, not your mom and dad's Christmas function. I mean . . . that's the mayor. And I recognized Principal Hammer from the high school."

"I think this is a pretty safe space. My parents keep the invite list to those they know and who don't run their mouths. Too much." Bozeman was expanding fast but the small-town roots grew deep.

"Really? That's actually amazing."

"Oh, don't get me wrong. They all talk amongst themselves, like we're doing. But it usually doesn't go further than this room." I scanned the crowd, loving that even though I'd been gone for so many years, it felt like coming home. "I missed this party. I missed Christmas in Montana."

"Violet told me you guys are moving home. Are you excited?"

"I am. It will be nice to be around my family. I'll be even more excited when Violet and I can get our own place. I just bought some property this week."

"When are you moving?"

"I haven't nailed down a date. I was hoping before the school year starts next fall. I need to get the satellite office up and running. Build a house. It would actually be easier to do all of that if I was here. Trying to do it from LA just makes it all harder and takes longer."

"You can't live with your parents for a while?"

I opened my mouth to tell her no but . . . why couldn't I live with my parents for six months? Their house was enormous. Violet and I had our own space, and they'd love having us under their roof. "Huh."

"Huh, what?"

"I'm wondering why I didn't think of moving here now."

She laughed. "Probably because it's the middle of the school year. Parents usually think about doing everything in the summer."

"True." Except why wait? It wouldn't take more than a phone call and some paperwork to enroll Violet in the

Bozeman school district. She wouldn't be excited about leaving her friends, but that feeling wouldn't change between now and next fall.

"Do you need to be in LA for work if your satellite office isn't ready?" Natalie asked.

"No, I can work from Bozeman. My team won't move until the office is ready, but if I was here, I could expedite that process. And I would like to be here during construction of the house."

"I assume your dad is building it for you."

I nodded. "That's the plan. Heath will run lead on it."

"And you can be here to help with the details. Violet can switch schools. You can work remotely. And both of you can enjoy Bozeman in the winter."

I stared at her, blinking twice. She made it seem so simple. I wanted to live here. So I should live here. "Then I guess . . . I guess I live here."

"You live here." She smiled. "Welcome home."

There wasn't a smile in the world as welcoming as Natalie's.

"I live here," I repeated. Saying it out loud made it all click. I lived here. This wasn't a trip to visit family for the holidays. We lived here. It was time for us to live here.

The to-do list in my head exploded.

First, I needed to get Violet enrolled in school. Then I'd need to arrange for some of our things to be sent up here next week. Clothes. Toys. Books. I'd probably need to take a quick trip to LA to make arrangements at the office.

My assistant could organize the actual move and getting the rest of our belongings packed. The nanny I had hired for after the holidays would need to be notified. Our home in LA needed to be put on the market.

I fought the urge to send my assistant an email tonight, knowing he'd drop everything, including his holiday plans, to dive in. Then I'd have to call Cece and tell her about the new timeline.

I swallowed a groan.

"Are you okay?" Natalie put her hand on my forearm. "Your smile disappeared."

"I was just thinking about Cece, my ex. She knows we're moving here but I haven't told her the details. It won't be a pleasant conversation telling her it's happening and happening immediately."

"Ah." Natalie nodded. "Will she fight you on it?"

"Exactly the opposite." I looked to my daughter, still standing beside Dad. Mom had joined them, and they were pointing out the best desserts. "Cece won't care. That's hard on Violet."

"Oh." Natalie cringed. "I'm sorry. For you and Violet."

"Cece was in Hawaii when we left to come here. I don't know if she's back or even remembers that it's Christmas. I haven't spoken to her in weeks and neither has Violet. Part of the reason we haven't come home for the holidays in recent years was because it was easier in LA. Easier for me to hunt down Cece and remind her to acknowledge Violet. But this year . . . I just needed to come home."

Montana was home.

"I can understand that."

"Before the divorce, we didn't come here often either. Cece doesn't like Montana. She gets bored."

"Bored? In Bozeman?"

"Not enough shopping or friends to entertain her," I explained. "She never got along well with my parents. The first couple of years after Violet was born, I was swamped with work and it was easier to stay at home. We came here one year and all Cece did was complain that it was too cold. In hindsight, I should have just come without her."

In hindsight, there were a lot of things I should have done differently where Cece was concerned.

"That put a damper on the conversation." I sighed. "Sorry. I don't talk about Cece much. Mostly because I know how she'll look at the end of the conversation."

"Like a spoiled bitch?"

"Pretty much." I chuckled. "I don't ever want people to run her down and risk the chance that Violet will overhear."

"My lips are sealed."

And what beautiful lips they were.

A waiter passed us with a tray of champagne flutes. I snagged two and held one out for Natalie.

"I'd better not." She waved it off. "I'm on the clock.

And speaking of such, I'd better get back to your daughter."

"She's fine with my parents."

"You're paying me to watch her."

"Would you feel better if I didn't pay you?"

"Actually, yes. It feels strange to be paid when I'm enjoying myself so much."

I held out the champagne again. "Done."

She took it and smirked. "You're still going to pay me, aren't you?"

"Yes." I tipped my flute to my lips and smiled. After a sip—my parents didn't skimp on the champagne and it was as delicious as it was expensive—I caught Mom's eye and motioned to Violet.

Mom waved, then nodded to Violet, mouthing, "I've got her."

"Thank you," I mouthed back, then took Natalie's elbow and steered her toward the door. "Consider this your break."

"I just had a break."

I grinned. "An extended break."

She sipped her champagne as I led her down the stairs to the lobby. Some of the crowd from earlier had cleared out and there wasn't as much bustle and noise. One of the tables beside a large window was open.

I walked over and pulled out a seat for her, then took my own. "I forgot how pretty this building is."

"I rarely make it here." She turned her blue eyes up to the star on the massive tree.

I traced the long column of her throat with my gaze, wishing I could trace it with my tongue instead. Wishing I could latch my mouth over her pulse and suck.

Christ. My cock swelled behind my zipper—again—and I drew in a long breath. There hadn't been a woman who'd stirred my blood in years. I hadn't even cared about women, and my fist had served me fine since my divorce. But Natalie . . .

I was fully under her spell.

"I don't want you to think that I do this," I told her.

Her gaze shifted to mine. "Do what?"

"Chase Violet's caretakers."

The corner of her mouth turned up. "Is that what you're doing? Chasing me?"

"I'd like to."

Her smile widened. "I think maybe we should table this conversation until my gig working for you is up."

"That would probably be the prudent decision. I can wait a week."

She lifted a shoulder. "We'll see."

"We'll see?" That wasn't the enthusiastic agreement I'd expected. She'd told me that she'd been into me in high school. That she'd had a crush. Was that where it had ended? I could have sworn she was into me but . . . "Did I read this wrong?"

"Maddox, you just decided to move here thirty

minutes ago. When you do, Violet will need your attention. And it sounds like there are a lot of lingering feelings where your ex-wife is concerned. So . . . we'll see."

Damn. Taking on a relationship at this point would be hard. I didn't have much extra to give. But for Natalie, it was tempting to find a way.

"You're right about Violet. She does need my attention. But where Cece is concerned, there are no lingering feelings. I fell out of love with her three years ago when we got divorced. Probably longer than that, if I'm being honest. The way she treated Violet . . . well, I couldn't love a woman like that."

"Can I ask you a very personal question that you have every right to ignore and tell me to mind my own business?"

"Of course." I grinned, doubting there was much I wouldn't tell her. Even tonight, after sharing a single dance, it was like my filter had disappeared.

"Cece sounds awful." Natalie made a sour face. "Why did you marry her?"

"Now you sound like my mother."

"Sorry. We don't have to talk about this."

"No, it's fine." I sighed and took a sip of my champagne. Talking about Cece was never easy but Natalie deserved the details. "She wasn't always awful. Or, I didn't see it. Cece is beautiful and vivacious. We met in college and she was that girl who everyone gravitated toward. She is always up for a party. Her laugh is infectious. And I was a young guy who had a lot happening and she made my life . . . lighter."

Natalie shifted, leaning her elbows on the table. She listened, intently. During the party. On the dance floor. Even in a room full of people, she listened. It was addictive, having Natalie's focus.

Cece had always kept one ear on the activity, sparing the bare minimum to conversation unless it was about her. And she would have never let me steer her away from the party.

"When we got together, I was just starting Madcast," I said. "I was working my ass off to graduate and get the company off the ground. Cece would haul me out of my house and take me to a bar and we'd have a blast for a few hours. At the time, I needed that. I asked her to marry me before graduation. We got married not long after. And things were good. Until . . . ."

"Violet," she whispered and a little of the heartache I felt for my daughter was written on Natalie's face.

"Yeah." I nodded. "Cece was on birth control. She let a little too much time go between shots and got pregnant. Everything changed after that. Gone was the fun woman who'd added some levity to my life. She hated that I worked so much. Looking back, she had that right. As Madcast took off, I worked all the time. I only went to one of her doctor's appointments, and when she started having contractions, I was in a meeting and missed her calls, so she went to the hospital alone."

Natalie winced. "Ooof."

"Not my proudest moment."

"My dad always said it takes two to make a relationship work. Or not to work."

"He's right about that. I let Cece down. I won't blame the demise of our marriage entirely on her. But I will hold her responsible for how she's treated Violet. Our daughter is innocent. She's just a little girl. Cece might not have wanted to be a mother, but she *is* a mother."

"That's fair."

"One day, Cece decided we weren't what she wanted anymore. She didn't want to settle down. She'd been having an affair and fallen in love with a guy she'd met at the gym. Some model. That was the end. I can't even say I was upset. We'd been over for a long time before that. The divorce just made it official."

"And you fought for Violet."

"I always will." I nodded. "I've stayed in LA hoping that Cece will suddenly change, but I'm just fooling myself and making it harder on Violet. Cece travels. She's with the same guy. They hop all over the world, posting pictures of her glamorous life paid for by the money she made from giving me custody of Violet."

Natalie's eyes softened. "While you post pictures of Violet because she is the glamour in your life."

"Yes. I posted one yesterday of her blowing bubbles—"

"In the hot tub. I saw. It was so cute."

"You looked me up?"

"Absolutely. I stalked your Instagram earlier today. It's how grown women research handsome men these days. You really should make your account private."

I chuckled. "So noted."

"For the record, I think you're doing the right thing. Moving here. Creating a new life for Violet."

"Thank you." I saluted her with my champagne, then drained the rest of my glass.

Natalie did the same, and when she set her flute down, she gave me another one of those dangerous smiles.

"It's taking all of my willpower not to kiss you, just to see what it would feel like." The confession came out without any restraint or regret.

"Oh, it would be fantastic." She leaned in a little closer as she teased. "I'm really good at kissing."

"Of that, I have no doubt."

"But . . ." She shook her head. "I'm still your employee."

"I'm contemplating firing you."

She laughed, the sweet sound ringing through the lobby.

When was the last time I'd just talked to someone this openly? The only people who really knew what had happened with Cece were my parents and brothers. Sharing it with Natalie came as naturally as breathing. She was alluring and real and honest. With her, things seemed . . . easy.

I could use a little easy in my life.

A strand of hair fell across her cheek. I reached out and tucked it behind her ear, earning a small gasp as my fingertips brushed her skin.

Now that she'd caught my attention, I struggled to look away, even as a flash of red caught the corner of my eye.

Natalie was the most beautiful female I'd ever laid eyes on.

Except for the very pretty and very angry little girl marching our way.

CHAPTER SEVEN

NATALIE

"Hi. How was dancing?" I gave Violet a smile, expecting one in return. Instead, I got the death glare. The same one she'd sent me when I'd wrung my wet sweater out over her head on our first day together.

"What's wrong?" Maddox slid from his seat and took a step toward her.

Violet sent her glare his way, then spun around on a gold slipper and ran away.

What the hell? I stood, my mouth falling open.

"Violet!" Maddox called but she was already gone. "Shit."

He jogged in the direction she'd gone, toward one of the restaurants, and even though the crowd had thinned from earlier, there were still enough people that they swallowed her up.

I scurried in my heels to catch Maddox who was

blocked and slowed by a family coming out of the restaurant.

"What's going on?" I asked as I reached his side. I pressed in close to his arm, keeping pace as he squeezed by people and kept pushing forward.

"I don't know. I thought she was having fun." His head swept back and forth, searching for his daughter. "Violet!"

I inspected every piece of red I spotted, hoping it was her dress, but wherever she'd gone, she'd done it with the intention of disappearing. Why? What was wrong?

Maddox kept walking, down a hallway that led to an exit door. He tested the handle. Locked. "Damn it."

"She must have gone into the restaurant and we passed her." I turned and hurried back that direction, bypassing the hostess as I searched between tables. I weaved through them, seeing Maddox the next row over doing the same.

When we reached the wall of windows that over-looked Main Street, I found Maddox already backtracking.

Where would she go? Why would she run away from us? Had something bad happened at the party? Was it because I'd been sitting with her dad?

He didn't wait for me as he ran out of the restaurant, headed to the other across the lobby. I did one more sweep of the hostess station, checking beneath the counter, then rushed out, meeting Maddox at the base of the staircase.

"Anything?" he asked.

"No. What's going on?"

He raked a hand through his hair. "She does this."

"Does what? Run away?"

He sighed and nodded. "She gets mad at me or her feelings get hurt, and she'll run off and hide. But it's always at home. She's never done it in public before."

"Why? Was it because we were sitting together?"

"It has to be." The worry on his face cracked my heart. "Fuck."

"We'll find her. Where does she normally hide at home?"

"I don't know. I've never found her. She hides and comes out when she's ready. One night, she hid for six hours."

"Oh, hell," I muttered and looked around the lobby. We did not need Violet hiding here for six hours.

If she had backtracked and snuck away from us, she probably would have gone upstairs. She might be mad, but she'd likely stay close to the party where there were familiar faces mixed in with the strangers.

"We'll find her." If we had to interrupt the party and enlist the guests to help, then so be it. "We'd better divide and conquer."

Maddox nodded. "You go upstairs and start searching there. I'll talk to the managers of the restaurants and see if they'll let me into the kitchens. It wouldn't shock me if she snuck in with the waitstaff."

"Good idea." I spun and hurried up the staircase toward the party.

There were so many people in the ballroom it was nearly impossible to see if she'd gone in there, but I did a lap around the outer edge of the space, looking between legs and under tables. When I saw no sign of her or her red dress, I hit the dessert table and loaded up a plate with the biggest piece of chocolate cake I could find.

So far, sugar and bribery had been key with Violet. There was no point in changing tactics now.

My stomach twisted as I walked out of the ballroom, glancing down the staircase. Maddox stood beside the last step, talking to a woman in a pantsuit. There was so much fear and anxiety written on his face that it hurt to look at him as he spoke.

"Violet, where are you?" I headed for the hallway across from the ballroom. Thankfully, The Baxter wasn't a huge hotel. The top floors were only accessible with an elevator keycard, meaning she couldn't have gone too far.

Unless she'd snuck in with someone who had a card.

"She wouldn't do that." *Would she?*

Violet and I had been doing so well. Then I'd screwed up by flirting with Maddox. And I knew better, damn it.

I knew better.

How many women had Cathy fired over the years for this very thing? Three or four? There was a professional line I should never have crossed, no matter who the man was.

The first door down the hallway opened to a sitting room. When Violet and I had explored earlier, she'd peeked inside. Maybe she'd crawled under one of the couches. I pushed the door open, glancing inside, but instead of seeing Violet, I found Stella.

And her bare breasts.

"Oh my God." I tore my eyes away. "Sorry."

Stella gasped and pushed at the broad-shouldered man whose mouth was latched on to a nipple. Then she scrambled to right her dress as the man glanced over his shoulder.

"Natalie?"

"Heath?"

I looked between the two of them, my mouth hanging loose. "I wasn't here. I didn't see anything. You two, um . . . have fun."

My face was aflame as I closed the door. Better me walk in on them than Violet.

I moved to the next room—the men's restroom. I eased the door open and carefully peeked inside. The urinals were empty but I checked the toilet stalls too.

The bathroom's door swung open as I was checking the last stall, and I spun around, nearly spilling the cake in my hand.

"Uh . . ." The man coming in had already unzipped. His entire body froze when he spotted me.

"Sorry." I avoided any and all eye contact as I walked past him, keeping my gaze on the floor and not the organ peeking out from a pair of green silk boxers. "Wrong bathroom."

The women's restroom was my next stop. There were no ladies at the sink and the first three stalls were empty, but the last one's door was closed.

I crouched, looking for a pair of shoes. There were no feet dangling from the toilet, so I shifted, peering through the small gap by the door's lock.

And there it was.

Red.

Thank God.

I sighed and walked to the counter, hopping up on its edge. If it took more than two minutes to flush Violet out, I'd drag her out of here if necessary. Somewhere in the hotel, Maddox was worrying. But I'd rather avoid a scene and the chance of completely alienating this little girl.

So I took the fork I'd put on the plate with my cake and dove in, refusing to think about eating in a public bathroom. At least this one was clean.

"Yuuuuum," I moaned and chewed. "This is the best cake I've ever had in my life. It's new. They just put it out on the dessert table. Want to come out here and have a bite?"

Silence.

"Suit yourself. I'll eat it. It's so good, I doubt there will be any left when we go back to the party. It's got fudge frosting."

Silence.

Wow, this girl was stubborn.

I forked another huge bite and let out another moan. "So. So. Good."

The rustle of a skirt and the click of shoes on floor tiles before the door squeaked open.

"You're gross." She harrumphed and crossed her arms over her chest.

"Gross? Why am I gross?"

The tiara had come loose somewhere during her escape and was askew on her updo. She'd never looked more adorable. And sad. My heart ached for the sad. "You're just like all of the other nannies. All you want to do is kiss my dad. That's *gross*."

So she'd stormed off because I'd been talking with Maddox. And because I did want him to kiss me. *Shit*.

I set the plate aside and jumped off the counter. "Do a lot of nannies have crushes on your dad?"

"All of them," she muttered.

"Want to know a secret?"

She didn't answer but there was a flicker of interest in her expression.

I waved her over, then gave her the cake as a peace offering.

She took it and went to the counter, trying to climb up between the sinks to sit like I'd been. But with the height and her dress, she couldn't boost herself up.

"Let me help." I hoisted her up, and when I had her seated with the cake on her lap and a bite in her mouth, I resumed my own perch, hooking my ankles together and letting my feet swing.

The room had been designed so that as the door opened, anyone passing down the hall couldn't peer inside and see anything but a tiled partition. It wasn't the most elegant of places to talk, but with just the two of us in there, it was at least private and quieter than taking her to the ballroom.

"What's your secret?" she asked, her cheeks bulging and a chocolate crumb on her lip.

"I had a major crush on your dad when he was just a kid. All of the girls did."

"You knew Daddy as a kid?"

"In high school. When we were teenagers. I went to school with him and your uncles. Did you know that?"

She shook her head.

"Your dad was a nice boy. And now he's a nice man. Girls usually get crushes on the nice ones."

"Boys are weird."

"Yes, they can be weird." I laughed. "But someday you'll meet a nice one and maybe have a crush on him."

Her face twisted and she looked at me like I'd cracked.

"I do have a crush on your dad, Violet. That doesn't have to be a bad thing. And it doesn't have to mean anything. I'm still your nanny and your friend."

"He loves my mom." There was no confidence in her voice as she spoke the words, only the heartache of a girl who hadn't quite come to terms with her parents' split.

My chest ached because once upon a time, I'd been that little girl too. "I don't know how your dad feels about your mom, honey. Have you asked him?"

She shook her head, using the fork to poke at the cake. "She didn't send me a Christmas present. I checked under the tree and all of my presents are from Dad and Nana and Papa."

Ouch. Yeah, Cece was a bitch. No wonder Maddox was so frustrated with her. "Do you miss her?"

Violet shrugged. "She didn't come and see me at Christmas last year either. She promised to take me ice skating and lied."

I'd been around enough seven year olds to know that a broken promise was equivalent to a lie. And they delivered the biggest hurt. "Does she lie a lot?"

"All the time." Her chin started to quiver. "Now we're moving here and she's never going to see me."

I was off the counter and in front of her before her first tear fell. Taking the plate and setting it aside, I wrapped my arms around her and pulled her close as she cried.

"I'm sorry," I whispered when her breathing evened out except for the occasional hiccup. "Can I tell you another secret?"

"Yeah." She leaned away and the sadness on her face was familiar agony. This girl was breaking my heart.

"I only had a dad when I was your age."

"What happened to your mom?"

I swiped my thumb across her cheek. "I think maybe she was like your mom."

"Oh." Her chin fell.

My mother had left Bozeman when I was five, moving to North Carolina with the man she'd been sleeping with behind my father's back. Of course, I hadn't realized that at the time. Not until Dad had told me the truth on my fifteenth birthday.

When Mom had left Montana, she'd taken everything important with her except a little girl.

And an old 1969 mint-green Volkswagen bus.

Magdalena.

That bus was all I had left of my mother. Maybe it was foolish to cherish it like I did, but it was more mine now than it had ever been hers.

"There are moms like ours in the world," I told Violet. "I'm sorry you got one of them. But girls like us are lucky too."

"How?"

"Because even though we don't have the best moms, we have the very best of the best of the best dads. Don't you think?"

"I guess," she murmured.

She'd see, later in her life. She'd realize that Maddox adored her and would do anything to ease some of the pain.

"Want to know something else cool?" I asked, earning a nod. "I have a mom now. And she's the best of the best of the best. Her name is Judy. She became my mom when I was twenty."

"Twenty?" Ancient to a little girl.

"Yep. I was twenty. She met my dad at a restaurant in town. Dad and Judy started talking and then they started dating. And kissing."

"Kissing is gross."

I giggled. "Judy and my dad kiss *all* the time."

"Eww."

I pushed a lock of hair off her forehead. "I'm okay with the kissing because she married Dad and asked if she could be my mom. I love her a lot. Do you know why I love her so much?"

"Why?"

"She makes the most amazing chocolate cake. Better than this one." I tapped her plate. "She always remembers Christmas presents. And because she loves my dad with her *whole* heart."

Judy had never married or had children before she'd met Dad. She'd told me once that she'd come to terms with her life as a *spinster*—Judy loved her Regency romance. But it just hadn't been her time. She'd been waiting for Dad to find her. She was younger than him by a decade, but because of their love, I believed in soul mates.

"Judy makes my dad happy, and since all he ever wants is for me to be happy, I feel the same way about him. Like a circle. We want what is good for each other. Does that make sense?"

"Yeah." Violet nodded.

"I think that's all your dad wants for you. Just to make sure you're happy. Maybe someday, you'll be okay if he finds his own Judy."

She thought on it for a long minute, her forehead furrowed. "Are you a Judy?"

"No, I'm a Natalie. And though your dad is nice and I still have a teensy, tiny crush on him, right now I think we should not worry about Judys and go find him. He was freaked out when you ran away."

"Very freaked out." A deep, soft voice came from the doorway. Maddox strolled inside, and whatever fear he'd worn in the lobby was nearly gone, probably because he'd been listening at the door for a while.

"Sorry, Daddy." Violet flew across the bathroom, a streak of red, shooting into her father's arms.

He picked her up and held her tight, letting out a long breath and closing his eyes. "Never again, Violet. Don't you ever run away from me again. You scared me. If something happened to you . . . never again. Promise."

"I promise." She nodded and buried her face into his shoulder. "Sorry."

He held her tight, then let her go and set her on the floor. "Want to dance with me? You haven't danced with me tonight."

She nodded and took his hand, letting him escort her out of the bathroom.

I picked up the plate of decimated cake and followed, giving Maddox a wink when he glanced over his shoulder.

"Thank you," he mouthed.

"You're welcome," I mouthed back.

The party guests were none the wiser to our drama. Music blared and people laughed, enjoying their Christmas Eve.

Maddox took Violet straight to the dance floor, twirling her twice before picking her up and touching his nose to hers. Then he danced with her through the crush of couples, not once letting her feet touch the floor.

He was a good dad. The best of the best of the best.

And he needed her more than I wanted him.

The decision to stay away was the right one. Timing was not on our side. So with that resolution in mind, I went to my happy place.

The dessert table.

Eating one last piece of chocolate cake, making tonight the most sugar-filled night of the year—not even on Halloween when I ate one piece of candy for every twenty that I handed out could top this.

Judy was on a health kick at the moment, even through the holidays, and she'd warned me there'd be no chocolate cake after our Christmas dinner tomorrow. So tonight I indulged, in the sweets and in Maddox, watching from my spot against the wall as he danced with his daughter.

Hours later, midnight chimed on the grandfather clock

in the hallway and people slowly began to drift out of the ballroom.

Maddox hadn't let go of Violet the rest of the night. The fright from earlier had rendered me useless. When I'd offered to take over, he'd told me he had her. When I'd told him I'd leave, he'd asked me to stay close.

Violet seemed to have forgiven me. She'd even held my hand while people had come to talk to her father. Maybe she'd scared herself a bit too with that stunt.

Around one o'clock, she began to yawn. Maddox picked her up, holding her like she weighed nothing while he continued visiting. And with the deep murmur of his voice, she drifted off against his shoulder.

"She's out," I told him, yawning too. "I don't blame her. I'm an early bird, not a night owl. I think I'll take off, unless you need me to stay."

"No, we'll get out of here too."

I followed them out of the ballroom, smiling at Hannah and Keith who stood sentry by the doors, bidding farewell to their friends.

Maddox kissed his mother's cheek. "See you at home."

I collected my coat from the check room where I'd left it earlier, and shrugged it on, pulling my car keys from my pocket.

"Brr," he said, wrapping his jacket around Violet as we stepped outside.

Fresh snowflakes fell from the dark sky. They quieted the street and blanketed the sidewalk.

It was magical. The perfect scene for a farewell.

"Thank you for inviting me tonight."

"Can we give you a ride home?" he asked.

I jingled my keys. "I'll be fine."

The white specks of snow clung to his dark hair. The faint streetlights made his features stronger. More handsome. His blue eyes were like sapphires, glowing bright as he stepped closer.

Foolish as it was, I hoped for a kiss. Just one before I walked away.

His breath tangled with mine in white wisps in the frozen air. He leaned in and my heart leapt. Then his lips were there, the faintest brush against mine before he was gone. "Merry Christmas."

"Merry Christmas."

I smiled at him, then looked to Violet, sleeping happily in her father's arms.

I wouldn't fall for a client. Not again.

And for her, I'd walk away.

So I took one step backward, then another and whispered, "Goodbye, Maddox."

CHAPTER EIGHT

MADDOX

I checked the time on my phone for the hundredth time. Where was Natalie? She should have been here by now. I'd hoped that maybe she'd come early since we hadn't seen her yesterday. She'd been on my mind constantly since the party, even with the flurry of Christmas activity—Violet's toys and gifts and meals—and I was anxious to see Nat's smile.

"What are you looking at?" Mom asked, coming to stand by my side at the front window.

"The snow," I lied.

She laughed. "Sure, son. If snow is how you think of Natalie."

"If you knew, why ask?"

"Because I'm your mother and forcing you to squirm is one of my job descriptions."

I chuckled and put my arm around her shoulders. "Are

you working today?"

"I've got a few things to hammer through in the office, but no. I'm going to try and take most of the day off. Your brother said something about watching the last season of *State of Ruin* already."

"He was supposed to keep that a secret."

"You have met Heath, haven't you? Despite what he thinks, he's never been able to keep a secret."

"I'll email you the link and login."

She smiled. "It's so good to have you home."

Home. "It's good to be here."

"Are you sure you're okay with us staying here?"

"I wouldn't have it any other way."

When I'd pulled Mom and Dad aside yesterday after breakfast and asked if they'd be okay with my accelerated move date, both had been ecstatic. When I'd offered to move into a condo in town, they'd both scoffed and insisted Violet and I stay right where we were. And since I was going to attempt life without a nanny, Mom had promised to help with Violet.

But first, we had a few days left with Natalie. If she'd get here already. I hadn't been this excited to see a woman in years. She made me smile effortlessly. She made me hang on her every word. And she was a miracle worker with my daughter.

When I'd eavesdropped on their conversation in the bathroom at the hotel during the party, I'd had a hard time breathing as Natalie had spoken. Not because of the story about her own mom, but because no woman had ever spoken to Violet that way.

Like a mother.

Not Cece. Not Mom—who'd always tried her best but she would always be a grandmother, prone to saying *yes*.

The crunch of tires on snow sounded outside, and I let Mom go, leaning closer to the window.

"Oh, Maddox." Mom laughed. "Don't lick the glass."

I shot her a scowl, then narrowed my eyes at the unfamiliar car coming down the lane.

That wasn't Natalie's Subaru. And it wasn't Natalie behind the wheel.

"Expecting someone?" I asked Mom.

"No." She shook her head and went to open the door.

We stood together, watching as an older woman stepped out of a gray sedan and walked our way.

"Good morning." She smiled brightly, extending her hand my way. "I'm Cathy Caron."

The owner of the agency where Natalie worked.

"Hi . . . Cathy." I shook her hand and waved her inside out of the cold. Then we stared at each other, that awkward silence hanging over our heads until Mom cleared her throat and excused herself.

"Should we start with an introduction to Violet?" Cathy asked.

I blinked and rubbed my jaw. "I'm sorry, Cathy. Forgive me for the confusion. What are you doing here?"

"Oh, sorry." Her smile dropped. "You must not have received my email."

"No." I hadn't logged in this morning, and over breakfast, while I normally checked email, I'd played a rock, paper, scissors tournament with Violet instead. "I apologize."

"That's my fault." Her façade cracked as her shoulders slumped and she smoothed the hair from her face. "It's been a hectic morning."

"Where is Natalie?"

"She's not coming. And I didn't have anyone else available over Christmas, so I came instead."

I didn't hear much of her explanation other than Natalie wasn't coming. "Is Natalie sick?"

"No, she's . . . unavailable."

Oh, shit. Had she gotten fired? Because of me?

I opened my mouth but nothing came out. What the hell did I say? Did Cathy know about my feelings for Natalie? How? I wasn't even sure exactly how I felt. "I, um . . ."

The last time I'd been this speechless had been when Violet had run away from one of her nannies in LA, locked herself in my bedroom and proceeded to remove the laces from my shoes and tie them together in one long string.

When I'd asked her why, she'd told me that she'd been planning to tie one end to the bed post and use the other to climb out a window. Granted, the laces combined had only been about eight feet long and my bedroom had been on the first floor, but her plan had been insane, albeit fairly well-thought-out.

"Yes?" Cathy asked.

"Nothing." I swallowed my disappointment and waved her deeper into the house. "Welcome. Thanks for coming. Violet was just in her room. Please, make yourself at home and I'll get her."

Cathy nodded and unzipped her coat.

I took the stairs two at a time and strode down the hallway to Violet's room, finding her on the bed with the Nintendo. I'd bought her a new game for Christmas and she was on a mission to dominate within the first forty-eight hours.

Maybe it would distract her today, so we didn't have a wreck with a new nanny.

"Hey, princess. Can you come to the living room? I'd like to introduce you to someone."

"Who?" She didn't look up from her Nintendo.

"There's a new nanny here to play with you today while I'm working."

Her fingers stopped moving. Her eyes lifted to mine. "Where's Natalie?"

"She's not coming today."

"Why?"

Because I fucked up. "I don't know," I lied. "I'm sorry."

Violet stared at me for a long moment, then huffed and put her game aside.

The introduction to Cathy went about as well as

expected. I showed her around the house while Violet begrudgingly followed. But she didn't throw a fit. Maybe that was because Cathy was in her fifties.

Violet's outburst at the party had been eye-opening. How was it that I could run a multi-billion-dollar business, but I didn't have a clue how to read my own child?

The nannies we'd had over the years had always been younger women. I assumed that was typical—my colleagues in California had caretakers around the same age. Sure, there'd been times when a former nanny had stood too close. Had laughed or blushed too often. I hadn't thought much about it because I hadn't considered any of them attractive. Who cared if they had a crush? I hadn't thought twice about a single one in that way.

Until Natalie.

But Violet had seen it all along while I'd been oblivious to just how much she noticed. And just how much it had bothered her.

"Do you have any special instructions?" Cathy asked as we ended the house tour.

"No. My parents have a chef here for the week, so he'll have lunch and snacks prepared. I have a meeting outside the house this morning but please call if you have any questions. My mother and father are around here somewhere. Violet can track them down if needed." I smiled at my daughter, earning a pout.

That pout actually made me happy. That pout meant she wanted Natalie here as much as I did.

So why the hell wasn't she here? I'd come on strong at the party but she hadn't seemed to mind. She'd put her boundary in place too, one I'd respected.

Damn it.

I knelt and took Violet's hand. "Have fun today. I love you."

"Love you too," she mumbled.

"Thanks, Cathy."

She smiled and nodded. "My pleasure."

Leaving her with Violet, I retreated to the office for my first call with the office in LA. I broke the news to my assistant about my expedited move first. As expected, he immediately got to work and promised to do whatever necessary to make it a seamless transition.

After that call, I spoke with my general counsel and the head of human resources who informed me that one of our employees had been leaking content to Russian piracy sites.

Then I spoke to my CFO who reported that our actual revenue numbers as we approached year-end would be higher than the projections. But even with that good news, I was stuck on Natalie's absence.

Where was she? It had been a while since I'd flirted with a woman, but she'd flirted back, hadn't she? Why wasn't she here? Why hadn't she called?

By the time my conference calls for the morning were finished, I was late getting out of the house for my meeting with Tobias.

Holiday Homes was closed the week between Christmas and New Year's, so when I pulled into the parking lot ten minutes late, my Audi and Tobias's GMC were the only vehicles around.

Tobias was leaning against the empty reception desk, staring off into space, when I walked through the door.

"Hey." The scent of strong coffee and sawdust clung to the air. "Smells like Dad's old office in here."

Tobias nodded. "Brand-new building and it smells like the old one. But I like that."

"Me too." I shook his hand. "Thanks for meeting today."

The rest of my week was slammed, and this was the only free spot I had to talk construction plans. The second that property was officially mine, I wanted the permits approved and the crew ready to break ground.

Tobias would be designing my home because I wanted the best architect in town.

"Want some coffee?" he asked, leading me toward the break room.

"Sure." I followed, taking in the office. Dad had built it three years ago and today was only my second visit. "This is nice."

"You know Mom and Dad."

They'd declared a few years ago that they were going to spend some money. They'd worked their asses off their entire lives, teaching us boys how to do the same. And now they were reaping the benefits.

A custom home. New office buildings. Travel. Dad had bought Mom a three-carat Tiffany diamond ring for Christmas because the jewel in her original wedding ring was beginning to dull. Mom had bought Dad a five-thousand-dollar Bremont watch because he was always letting his phone run out of power and never knew what time it was.

The watch was almost identical to one Cece had bought me our last year together. She'd always been one to splurge on the holidays. For me. For Violet. For herself.

At the base of our tree, she'd have a mountain of gifts. After the divorce, I'd gotten rid of the gaudy watches and cufflinks she'd bought me over the years because none of them had meant a thing.

What I wanted was a woman who bought me a gift because she knew how much I'd love it, not simply because the price tag was five digits. I wanted gifts to make me smile. To make me laugh.

I could use more laughter in my life.

And from the look on Tobias's face, he could too.

"You okay?" I asked as he walked into his office and took a seat behind his desk. He'd been quiet yesterday through the Christmas festivities. I'd thought it was just because there was so much activity, but even now when we were alone, he seemed just as distant.

"Yeah." He rubbed his bearded jaw. "Great."

Not great. "Missed you at the party at The Baxter."

"Yeah. Had something come up." His eyes were unfocused as he stared at his desk.

"Tobias."

He swallowed hard.

"What happened?"

"Nothing."

"Talk to me."

Between Tobias and Heath, it was Tobias who I'd lost touch with the most. He'd been busy in college and working afterward. And I hadn't made time to keep in touch with my brothers.

With Heath, it hadn't mattered. He'd made up for my shortcomings over the years. Not a week had gone by since I'd moved away from Montana where he hadn't texted me at least once.

But Tobias and I had begun to drift apart. I hoped to make up for that now that I was home.

"I've been a shit older brother as of late. Give me the chance to make up for it."

The color drained from his face as he turned to stare blankly at the wall. "Do you remember Eva?"

"I never met her, but yeah." Eva had been Tobias's girlfriend through college. I wasn't sure exactly why they'd broken up, but according to Heath, it had wrecked him for a time.

Mom had always loved Eva, and during one of her regular phone calls—the ones where she'd gossip about my brothers—she'd told me how much she wished they'd get back together.

"She came over the other morning," Tobias said. "Christmas Eve."

"Okay," I drawled. "Are you getting back together or something?"

"No." He rubbed his hands over his face, then dropped the bomb. "She's pregnant."

"Oh." *Shit.*

"We hooked up a while back. The condom broke. She's pregnant. And she's moving to London."

Four statements, delivered with no inflection. Like he didn't have a clue how to deal with a single one. Before I could think of something to say, Tobias shook his head and picked up a pencil from his desk. "Let's go through what you want for your house."

"We can do this another day."

"No, today's good." He slid a notebook under the graphite tip and waited.

"Tob—"

"Five bedrooms? Or would you like six?"

I sighed, not wanting to push. "Six. And one in the guesthouse."

"Bathrooms?"

We spent the next hour discussing the house. Tobias asked questions and I answered. When he was done, before I could bring up Eva again, he stood from his desk.

Meeting adjourned. "I'll get a preliminary draft sketched and bring it over soon."

"Thank you." I nodded, taking the hint that it was time to go.

I'd give Tobias some time to adjust to the pregnancy news, then talk to him again. I wasn't going anywhere, not this time.

The minute I was in my Audi, I pulled out my phone, hoping to see a missed call from Natalie. The screen was blank. Where was she? Why hadn't she come today? My curiosity was driving me insane.

Fuck it. I sent a quick email to my assistant that something had come up and I needed him to reschedule my next two meetings. Then I dialed Heath's number.

"Hello?" he answered, his voice muffled.

"Are you still in bed?" It was after eleven.

"Maybe."

"I need a favor."

"What?" he yawned.

"Do you happen to know Natalie's phone number? Or her address?"

"Why do you need it? Isn't she working for you today?"

"Heath," I grumbled. "Do you have her number?"

"Hold on." There was a rustling sound, then I was put on mute.

"Christ, what am I doing?" If Natalie wanted to see me, she would have showed up at the house this morning.

The right thing to do would be respect her privacy and leave her alone. But did I hang up the phone? No. Because damn it, there was something different about her.

Maybe not different but . . . familiar. She wasn't fake like many women in the entertainment world—my world. She didn't seem interested in status. She was grounded and real. Being around her was like being blasted to the past, before Madcast. Before the money.

Before I'd left Montana.

I wanted to taste her lips. I wanted to feel her curves beneath my palms. I wanted to thread my fingers through her soft hair and devour her whole.

I wanted her more than I'd ever desired a woman.

The silence on the other end of the phone ended abruptly. "Maddox?"

"Still here."

"I guess Natalie lives in the house where she grew up."

"With her father?"

"No, I think she bought it from him. Or something. I'm not sure. But do you remember where it is?"

"Vaguely, but a specific address would be good."

"I don't have one. It's in our old neighborhood. Dark green house two blocks over."

"Which direction?" I clenched my teeth.

"Uh . . . toward the elementary school?"

"You're killing me."

"Dark green isn't that popular of a color. You'll find it. How many could there be?"

Two. There were two dark green homes on the street that was two blocks away from my childhood home.

The first of the two dark green homes was occupied by a *lovely* older woman—Christine—who'd threatened to sic her Pomeranian—Roxy—on me if I didn't *get my soliciting ass off her front porch.*

Apparently in faded jeans and a black sweater, I resembled a door-to-door solicitor.

At the second dark green house, I figured I was in the right spot when I read the welcome mat.

The Neighbors Have Better Stuff.

I chuckled as I stood outside Natalie's home, uninvited. Before I could knock or ring the bell, the door whipped open and there she was with a houseplant tucked into the crook of one arm.

"Hi."

She blinked those beautiful blue eyes. Twice. "H-hi."

"You didn't show up today."

Her shoulders fell and she held out the plant. "I'm sorry. This is my apology aloe. I was leaving to bring it over and say goodbye."

"Apology aloe." I took the pot from her hands. "Never heard of it."

"It doubles as a Christmas present and a housewarming gift. They're very useful if you have kids who are accident prone. Or kids who might attempt to melt their Barbies into zombies with a blowtorch."

She'd bought me a gift. An aloe plant. For my

daughter who might very well melt her Barbies into zombies with a blowtorch.

I threw my head back and laughed, the sound carrying down the block. God, it felt good to laugh. It felt good to know that she'd been on her way over. Yes, she'd come over to say goodbye, but we'd deal with that word later.

"What are you doing here?" she asked.

I answered by stepping forward, forcing her inside. With the aloe plant set on the floor, I closed the door behind me and moved into her space. Before she could retreat out of my grasp, I framed her face with my palms. "I met Cathy."

Her shoulders slumped. "Yeah."

"You're not my nanny anymore."

"No, not anymore." Her mouth turned down. "Sorry."

"I'm not."

Then I kissed the sad look off her face.

CHAPTER NINE

NATALIE

B est. Kiss. Of. My. Life.

Of course Maddox Holiday could kiss. He'd barely kissed me after the party and I'd thought about it all day yesterday. That had been nothing more than a touch. Whatever expectations I'd had were destroyed with one sweep of his tongue across my bottom lip.

Maddox's hands stayed firm on my face, holding me against his mouth as I melted into a puddle.

My knees weakened. A moan escaped my throat.

He took advantage and slid inside, his taste exploding on my tongue. The heat from his mouth was heady. A dizziness washed over me as his mouth slanted over mine. So lost in the feel of him, I just stood there. Motionless. Stupefied. A woman on the verge of becoming goo.

Was this a dream? Maybe I was dreaming. *Kiss him back*. Why wasn't I kissing him back?

Before I had the chance to tangle my tongue with his, he pulled away, dropping his forehead to mine.

No, I was just getting ready to kiss him back.

"Natalie, I—"

"Kiss me again," I blurted, then rose up on my toes and tossed my arms around his shoulders, holding on tight.

He didn't miss a beat. He slammed his mouth down on mine and whatever sweetness had been in that first kiss morphed into sinful, delicious lust. Maddox devoured me, his tongue dueling with mine.

My fingers dove into the thick strands of his hair, tugging and toying while I poured everything I had into this kiss.

If this was all I'd have of Maddox Holiday, damn it, I was going to make an impression. For us both.

Maddox's arms banded around my back and he picked me up off my feet, carrying me to the nearest wall.

My legs wrapped around his narrow hips as he pressed my spine against the surface. I clung to him, my mouth never leaving his. We kissed for what felt like hours, until my core throbbed and I ached for more.

He arched his hips, digging his arousal into my center for one blissful second before he tore his mouth away. "Fuck."

"Yes, please."

Maddox shook his head. "I wanted to kiss you on Saturday. But this . . . damn, you can kiss, Nat."

Oh, thank God. If the only thing I achieved in this life

was Maddox thinking I was a good kisser, I'd die a happy woman. "I used to practice on my arm when I was a teenager."

He grinned and set me down on unsteady legs. "What else did you practice when you were a teenager?"

"That's for me to know and you to find out. Though let's just say it involved a banana."

"Natalie," he groaned. "You're killing me here."

"What? I make excellent banana bread. Someone told me once that men loved banana bread."

He threw his head back and laughed.

What a sight he was when he laughed. It transformed his face from the stoic businessman to this blindingly beautiful man.

When he looked at me again, he was still laughing, the dimple on full display. Because I might not have another chance, I reached up and touched it with a fingertip.

Maddox's fingers threaded through the hair at my temples. "Why didn't you come today?"

"Because as much as you wanted to kiss me on Saturday, I wanted it ten times over. I couldn't do that to Violet. She needs you. And . . ."

The truth was so freaking embarrassing. I didn't really want to tell Maddox about the past, but I didn't want him to find out from any other person.

"And what?"

"I've made this mistake before," I admitted with a cringe. "I can't do it again."

"Again?" His forehead furrowed. "With a father?"

I sighed and walked past him, leading the way to the living room couch.

He followed, sitting beside me.

"When I was eighteen, I started working for a single dad. Deacon," I said, keeping my eyes trained forward on the coffee table. Not many knew this story because it was humiliating. "He had twin boys who were seven. His divorce was new, or so I'd thought. Deacon's ex-wife wasn't around much but the boys talked about her all the time. I didn't think a thing of it because I never saw her at the house. I assumed she just lived in town."

When it came to the twins, I'd only ever dealt with Deacon. He'd been at the house to greet me each morning before leaving for work, and he'd been home every night at five-thirty so I could go home before dinner.

"It was just for the summer. It was more like babysitting and my first full-time job before I'd gone to work for Cathy. I was watching the twins while school was on break."

"He wasn't divorced, was he?"

I shook my head. "No, he wasn't. His wife was a journalist and she'd been given an assignment in Italy for the summer. I didn't know."

Maddox put his hand on my shoulder. "Nat, this isn't on you."

"I know." I gave him a sad smile. It had taken me years to realize that I'd been Deacon's prey. He'd been a handsome, older man who'd known exactly what to say to lure me into his bed. I'd slept with that man three times before learning that his wife had been out of town but very much still his wife.

I'd kept the affair a secret for a few years, finally admitting it to Judy after she'd married Dad. Cathy knew too because I'd wanted to be completely up front with her when I'd applied to work for her agency.

Otherwise, no one knew and I was certain that Deacon wasn't gossiping. Last I heard he was still married.

"When I found out about his wife, I quit immediately. The worst part was knowing that I'd betrayed those boys. They'd trusted me, and I'd gotten wrapped up in their father. He was a bastard for lying to me, but I should have known better. And that's on me. I can't go there again. Certainly not with you."

"With me?"

"I like you, Maddox. I've always liked you. I don't know if you want to explore this or not—"

"I do."

Relief coursed through my veins. "Then I can't be the nanny. Violet needs someone who's only about her. She deserves that."

"Agreed." He took one of my hands. "You're fired."

I laughed. "I already quit. And I have an apology aloe to prove it."

"Go on a date with me."

"But what about Violet?"

"She can find her own date."

I swatted his arm. "You know that's not what I mean."

"I know." Maddox shifted, inching closer. "But hear me out."

"Okay."

"Violet is and will always be my priority. Everything you just said about her needing someone that's only about her is right. And it's sexy as hell that you care enough about my daughter to walk away. But . . ."

He straightened, sitting taller. His gaze locked with mine and sheer determination was written on his face. This was the Maddox who led a billion-dollar company. This was the man in charge, ready to make his case.

Talk about sexy as hell.

"Violet doesn't have a lot of positive female relationships. She's had some great teachers. My mom. But thanks to Cece and her other nannies, she's seen a lot of women walk out of her life."

My hand pressed against my heart, aching for his girl. "I hate that for her."

"I hate that for her too." He gave me a sad smile. "I want her to know there are kind, caring women in this world. That you're one of them. So go on a date with me and spend time with Violet. It doesn't have to be one or the other."

"You are extremely convincing." A smile tugged at my mouth. "Do you always get your way?"

"Usually." He chuckled. "Is that a yes?"

"Yes." A date with Maddox. My heart skipped. "When?"

"Is tonight too soon?"

"Not really."

"Good. I'll pick you up at six."

"Actually, what if I came over? I feel awful for ditching Violet today and I have a present for her too." It was candy and a coloring book.

"Whatever you want." Maddox brought my hand to his mouth, kissing my knuckles. Then he stood. "I'd better get back. Make sure Violet hasn't chased Cathy out of the house. See you tonight?"

"Yes." I escorted him to the door with a smile so wide it pinched my cheeks.

"One more." He pulled me into his arms, kissing me again and giving me one more taste before leaving to go home.

I waited, watching from the threshold until his Audi was out of sight. Then I closed the door and screamed. "Ahh!"

Maddox had kissed me.

Maddox Holiday, the hottest man I'd ever known, had freaking kissed me.

I ran around the house screaming with my hands waving above my head. I was in the middle of a happy dance on the couch when the front door opened. My heart dropped to my feet as I shoved the hair out of my face, hoping above all hope that Maddox hadn't forgotten something and had decided to come back.

No, it was just my father. He didn't believe in knocking.

"What are you doing?" Dad gave me a sideways look. In his arms was the potted houseplant I'd left at his place yesterday.

"He kissed me." I hopped down from the couch. "I had to celebrate."

"Judy!" Dad bellowed over his shoulder.

"I'm right here, Garrett." She scowled at him as she shoved past him and stepped inside. "Do you always have to shout?"

Dad had two volumes. Loud and super loud. But his deep, boisterous voice always made me smile.

"She's talking about kissing," he said. "That's not my department."

I rolled my eyes. "You pretend like you didn't give me the sex talk when I was twelve."

"And I still have nightmares about that, so if we're celebrating you kissing someone, I'm out." Without another word, Dad set the plant on the tiled entryway beside my potted aloe, then backed out of the door, closing it behind him.

"We're celebrating a kiss?" Judy asked, taking off her coat.

"Yes." I jumped back up on the couch and did another shimmy. "Maddox kissed me."

I spent the next thirty minutes telling Judy everything, from my crush in high school, to being hired as Violet's nanny, to the party, to the kiss. When I was done, she texted Dad and told him it was safe to come inside—he'd been hanging out in the car, listening to a true crime podcast.

"So is he the reason you were in a bad mood yesterday?" Judy asked.

"I wasn't in a bad mood."

"Okay, not exactly bad. But you weren't yourself."

We'd spent Christmas together yesterday, per our tradition, eating and watching movies. I'd lazed the entire day away on Judy and Dad's couch. Maybe there'd been a little sulking too over Maddox and the phone call I'd had to make to Cathy to quit.

When I'd finally peeled myself off their couch at midnight, I'd trudged home, leaving my gifts behind—the snake plant Dad had brought over and a personalized recipe binder Judy had filled with her favorites. She was still holding out hope that one day I'd become a fantastic cook, like she was. She failed to forget that I'd once exploded a hot dog in the microwave.

"What are you wearing on your date?" Judy asked.

"I don't know yet."

"Do I know this guy?" Dad asked.

"Maddox Holiday."

He raised his eyebrows. "As in Madcast, Maddox Holiday?"

"The one and only." This was a fantasy. This was a dream.

"What's he like?" Judy asked.

"Nice. Smart. Sofreakinghot."

"Do I need to leave again?" Dad asked, hooking a thumb over his shoulder toward the door.

I smiled. "Maddox has a seven-year-old daughter and she's a spitfire. I sort of love that she isn't an angel."

Judy put a hand on Dad's leg, looking up to him with a smile. "I sort of love that your daughter isn't an angel either."

"What are you talking about? I'm an angel."

She scoffed as Dad studied a speck on his jeans.

"I've always been a good girl."

"Sweetheart, do you not remember how we met?" she asked.

"We met at dinner. In this house."

"Technically, yes. We had dinner. But the first time I saw you was when you were toilet papering the neighbor's yard."

"Whoa. Whoa. Whoa." I held up a hand. "You can't prove that was me."

Dad pulled his lips in to hide a smile.

In all the years since Judy had been a part of Dad's life, I had yet to, and would never, admit guilt of that night. Besides, it wasn't like I'd actually toilet papered Mrs. Henderson's yard. I'd simply ensured that she'd had an adequate TP supply since she'd kept sending her puppy over to poop on Dad's front lawn.

I'd been living at home at the time, saving money for when I decided to quit nannying and enroll at Montana State. Dad had brought Judy home after one of their early dates, wanting to introduce the two of us. An hour before they'd showed up, I'd come home and walked to the front door, texting and not paying attention. It had been dark and I'd been in my favorite pair of tennis shoes. My foot had splattered in a huge pile of fresh puppy shit.

That had been the final straw.

So I'd gone inside and decked myself out in head-to-toe black. Then I'd waited for the Hendersons' light to go off before staging my attack. It hadn't been your typical toilet papering. No, I'd scooped up every pile of puppy poo and made a little mountain of it in Mrs. Henderson's yard. Then I'd built a pyramid out of toilet paper beside it.

Because I *was* an angel.

The only actually toilet papering had been done to a shrub. The smallest shrub in her yard because I was nice like that. I'd been winding down that single roll when Dad and Judy had pulled into the driveway.

Dad had been talking about Judy nonstop for days, and the moment she'd stepped out of the car, laughing at something Dad had said, I'd panicked and raced down the block. I'd killed two hours in the elementary school playground waiting to make sure she'd gone home.

Two days later, when Dad had arranged a do-over

introduction, Judy had showed up with a pack of Charmin Ultra-Soft.

The next day, she'd come back, this time bearing homemade chocolate cake and I'd instantly given Dad my approval.

He'd married her four days later and they'd moved into Judy's house. Instead of selling this home to a stranger, he'd rented it to me so I wouldn't have to move.

Mrs. Henderson still lived next door. As far as I knew, she had no idea it was me who'd left the toilet paper. I'd cleaned it up the next day because I'd felt bad. Her dog still pooped in my yard. And I still piled it in hers.

"Any word on Magdalena?" Dad asked. He didn't love the bus, because it had been Mom's, but he also hadn't sold it because after Mom had abandoned me, I'd used Magdalena as my childhood fort. Then when I'd been old enough to drive, we'd gotten her working.

"No." I sighed and collapsed on the couch by his side. "I'm worried, Dad. What if they can't resuscitate her?"

"She's a car, kiddo."

I gasped and shot him a glare. "How dare you talk that way about Magdalena?"

"Do you need money for *Magdalena*?"

Yes. "No."

I'd planned to use the money made from watching Violet for the mechanic. But now that would have to wait. I could dip into my school savings, but I'd made myself a promise years ago when I'd started saving never to raid the college stash.

"I've been thinking about school."

Judy sat straighter, looking past Dad to my face. "And?"

"I think it's time. As much as I like watching kids, it's not the long-term goal." And maybe telling my dreams to Maddox, a man who was wildly successful, made me want to finally start chasing them.

To afford it all, I might need to sell Magdalena. An older-model Subaru like Dad's would be less expensive to maintain and more dependable in the winter.

Dependable. *Blech.*

"We're here for you." Dad smiled. "Whatever you need."

"Thanks." I rested my head on his shoulder.

"What time is your date?" Judy asked.

"Six."

"We're going to Costco," Dad said. "Want to come with us?"

"No, I'd better stay and get ready."

He checked his watch. "You have hours."

"There's a lot that needs to happen before a first date. I'll need to take another shower and wash my hair. Exfoliate. Shave my legs in case—"

"Come on, Judy." Dad bolted off the couch and strode for the door.

"You torture him." Judy laughed, standing to follow.

I giggled. "He makes it too easy."

We hugged goodbye, and then I did another victory lap around the house, dancing and cheering, before I spent the rest of the day on my laptop, going through the application for school.

When I had an hour left, I took my second shower for the day so I could wash my hair and shave my legs. Then I collected the aloe plant, Violet's bag of jellybeans and her book to take with me as I headed across town to meet Maddox.

The honeybees in my stomach swarmed when I pulled into the driveway. "I can't believe this is happening."

This was happening.

I was going on a date with Maddox.

I smiled as I walked to the stoop, reaching for the bell only to have the door yanked open before I could touch the button.

"Hey." Maddox was a vision, his dark hair finger-combed. He was dressed like he had been earlier in a pair of jeans and a black sweater. The dark color made the piercing blue of his eyes pop.

"Hi." I handed over the plant and came inside, shedding my coat. I'd opted for jeans too and high-heeled boots with a caramel sweater.

"You look beautiful." He kissed my cheek, lingering for a moment with his lips by my ear.

"Thanks." I leaned into him, dragging in the spicy scent of his cologne.

"Hi, Nat."

I pulled away from Maddox as Heath came striding through the entryway. "Hi."

"How's it going?"

"Good." I studied his face, wondering if he remembered that I'd caught him sucking Stella's nipples at the party.

If he did, we weren't going to talk about it, which was fine by me. "So are you here for game night?"

"Uh . . ."

"Slight change in plan." Maddox gave me a pained look. "Mom and Dad declared tonight family game night."

"*Mandatory* family game night," Heath said, raising a half-full tumbler. "But there is alcohol."

"You don't have to stay." Maddox's hand dragged along the back of my arm. His featherlight touch left a trail of tingles in its wake. "But if you're up for it . . ."

"I'm very competitive. And I show no mercy."

He grinned. "Bring it on, Buchanan."

An hour later, I was officially dominating the Holiday game night.

"Who invited you again?" Heath asked as he shuffled the cards.

"Me," Maddox grumbled, rearranging his short stack of chips. It was clear he was just as competitive as I was, and the fact that I'd just won a huge poker hand was grating on him.

After surveying the massive collection of board games, we'd all decided on a Texas Hold'em tournament so we could all play the same game. Hannah and Keith. Maddox. Heath. Violet. Tobias was nowhere in sight but I hadn't wanted to ask why he'd shirked the attendance mandate.

"How are we doing?" I asked Violet. She'd declared herself my teammate early on in the game. According to Maddox, she'd had a nice day with Cathy. Though she'd told me I was *funner*.

"Seventeen, eighteen"—the clay chips clinked together as she stacked them—"nineteen blue ones."

Blue chips were worth one hundred fake dollars and there were only thirty in play.

"Excellent." I sent Maddox a malicious grin.

He glowered as Heath dealt the next hand.

Hannah had lost out early and was perfectly content to be the cheerleader for Violet and me. Judging by chips stacks, Keith was in second place. Heath had a similar stack to his father's. And then there was Maddox, dead last.

"Where did you learn to play poker, Natalie?" Hannah asked.

"My dad and I love playing card games. He taught me how to play when I was a kid."

"He did a good job." Keith picked up his cards, then tossed them back to the table. "I fold."

I showed my cards—a two and a seven—to Violet. She shook her head and I tossed them down. "We fold too."

"Why are we even playing?" Heath asked. "We should just declare Natalie the winner and move on to something else."

"Agreed." Maddox tossed his cards down. "I vote for any other game besides poker."

"Can I pick, Nana?" Violet asked.

"Sure." Hannah took her hand and the two of them went to the cupboard, browsing the massive collection of board games.

Maddox stood from his chair and nodded for me to follow him into the kitchen.

I hurried after him, checking over my shoulder that we were alone.

He walked without hesitation to the pantry. Hannah had brought out an enormous spread for us to graze on during the games, so I had no idea how he could be hungry after all of that but I followed.

"What are you—"

He snatched my hand and tugged me into the tiny room, gripping the back of my neck with one hand while the other pulled the door shut. Then his mouth was on mine, his lips greedy. His hands threaded into my hair while mine roamed his chest, my palms dragging against the hard lines of his body.

A groan escaped his lips.

A mewl came from mine.

He pressed me against the pantry's shelves, his arousal digging into my hip. "Fuck, I've wanted to do that all night."

"Good, then do it again."

He obeyed, wrapping me in his arms as his tongue twisted and tangled with mine. I was practically climbing him when he tore his mouth away just as the door whipped open.

Please don't be Violet.

"There's someone here for you," Heath said quickly, then slammed the door shut.

"Damn." Maddox sighed. "This was not how I wanted our first date to go. Sneaking around in my parents' house. Sorry."

I laughed and stood on my toes to press a kiss to the corner of his mouth. "Don't be. I'm having a blast."

"I'm glad you're here. But tomorrow, let's try this again. Dinner. Just the two of us."

"It's a date." I smiled as he dragged his thumb across my mouth before stalking out of the pantry.

I followed behind him, almost through the kitchen when a laugh carried through the house. A laugh that made Maddox freeze midstride.

"What?" I asked, nearly colliding with his back.

He closed his eyes and his jaw clenched.

"Maddox."

The carefree, fluid grace in his body disappeared. When he took off for the living room, his shoulders were bunched, and his hands fisted by his sides.

I followed, not sure what the problem was until I heard a word that made my heart stop.

"Mommy!"

No. My stomach plummeted.

We walked into the living room to see Hannah and Keith glaring at their newest guest—their anger barely contained—as Violet threw her arms around a beautiful brunette.

The woman straightened when she spotted Maddox, keeping one hand on Violet's shoulder. "Hey, Mad."

Mad.

Yes. Yes, he was.

"Cece," he clipped.

"Merry Christmas."

"Christmas was yesterday."

She smiled, oblivious or purposefully ignorant to the tension in the room. But when her gaze drifted past Maddox to me, the smile vanished. "Who are you?"

I opened my mouth to answer, but Violet beat me to it. "That's Natalie. She's my nanny."

Cece huffed. "You always loved the nannies, didn't you, Maddox?"

Ouch. Well played, Cece.

So much for game night.

CHAPTER TEN

MADDOX

"What are you doing here, Cece?" I shut the office door behind us. Violet had a tendency to listen in, and I didn't want her hearing if we got into a fight.

Cece walked to the desk and perched on its edge. "It's Christmas. I wanted to see Violet."

"And you couldn't have called first?"

She crossed her arms over her chest. "Would you have hidden the nanny if I had? Seriously, Mad. Another nanny? Could you be more of a cliché?"

"No." I held up a finger. "We're not discussing Natalie."

Who I dated was none of Cece's business. She'd lost the right to explanations when she'd abandoned our daughter. Besides, she'd had her mind made up for years. This wasn't the first time she'd falsely accused me of sleeping with the nanny.

It wouldn't matter to her that Natalie had known our family for years. That she'd graduated with Heath and Tobias. Or that her tenure as Violet's caretaker had totaled two days and a party. Cece would never accept Natalie.

"Answer my question," I ordered. "What are you doing here?"

"I wanted to see Violet."

"And?"

"And nothing." She pursed her mouth into a firm line.

I waited, my hands fisted on my hips. There was more behind this visit than her wanting to see Violet. If that was the case, she would have gotten here in time for Christmas.

Cece's hazel eyes flickered to mine as I waited. We'd had this standoff many, many times, during our marriage and after. She was as transparent as the office's windows.

So I waited, the clock on the wall ticking as the seconds passed. I'd do this all night if I had to. Though the longest Cece had ever gone in one of our stare-downs had been three minutes.

She huffed and flung out a wrist. "God, I hate it when you just stare at me. Fine. I had to cut my holiday vacation short, okay? Rip and I broke up and the last place I wanted to be was California while he flaunts his new girlfriend all over Instagram."

Rip. The model. The moron.

Now this visit made sense. Cece had always come

rushing to Violet when there wasn't someone she'd deemed a better companion for her time.

I pinched the bridge of my nose. "You can't just show up whenever you feel it's convenient. You have to call first, like a guest."

"A guest?"

"Yes, you are in fact a guest."

"I'm her mother."

"Then fucking act like it," I barked.

She flinched.

Shit. I cringed, hoping like hell our daughter wasn't listening beyond the door.

Mom had pulled Violet aside when I'd told Cece to follow me to the office. With any luck, they were still in the living room. Natalie was probably home by now. A few snide comments from Cece and she'd all but bolted for the door.

It had physically hurt me to let Natalie leave tonight, but I wouldn't force her to endure what promised to be a disaster. Cece had claws, and though I suspected Natalie had enough bite of her own, I'd save the drama for another date. If there was another date.

Goddamn, I hoped she'd give me another date.

"We're not going to do this." I raked a hand through my hair. "Not again. You don't have the right to show up uninvited. You don't have the right to barge into my family's home. You can stay here tonight because it's late, but tomorrow you're in a hotel."

"A hotel?" Her jaw dropped. "You're kidding."

"No, I'm not kidding. I won't do this to Violet."

"You have no right—"

"I have every right!" I bellowed. "I have every right. The judge granted them to me, and if you'd bothered showing up at the hearing, you would have heard it too. Except money was more important than our child."

Cece stared at me, her eyes wide. Violet had inherited Cece's nose and the shape of her face. But otherwise, Violet was mine with blue eyes and dark hair. She was mine. And it was time to set new boundaries.

"We're moving here."

"You said it was a possibility after school was done for the year."

"It's happening. Now. We're not waiting for school to be out. I want to get Violet into the Bozeman school system as soon as possible. The move is effective immediately. We'll stay here with Mom and Dad until my own house is ready."

"You can't move—"

"I can. How many times do I have to tell you that? I can. You let her go for twenty-five million dollars."

Her face paled. "Maddox."

I'd never been this blunt and harsh with Cece before. Instead of brutal honesty, I'd pandered to her, hoping if I didn't make waves, she'd show up for Violet. Hoping that if I walked on eggshells, she'd keep at least one promise.

No more. Natalie had showed Violet more genuine affection and attention in days than Cece had in years.

"Did you bring her a Christmas present?" I asked.

The guilt on her face was enough of an answer but she launched into an excuse, typical Cece style. "I was in a rush to make my flight. I got home from Hawaii, swapped out some clothes and went straight to the airport. There was no time to shop."

In a rush to make her flight. I scoffed. It wasn't like she had to make it through security lines in time. She had a private fucking plane and a pilot who'd wait for her to swing into a store and buy a last-minute gift.

"Please don't be mad." She pushed off the desk and crossed the room. That famous pout of hers, the one that hadn't worked on me in years, was fixed on her face. "I'm sorry I didn't get a gift. I'll take Violet shopping tomorrow for whatever she wants. Hopefully I can find something other than a dollar store. Tell me there's at least a mall or something."

"Don't do that."

"Do what?"

"Turn up your nose at Montana. Bozeman is a fantastic town. You've been here before and you know there are some upscale shops downtown. And a mall. I won't have you tainting this place for Violet by being a snob. This is going to be her home."

She snarled. "Why are you being such an asshole tonight?"

"Do you really need me to answer that question?"

"Come on, Mad." Cece sighed, placing her hands on my chest. "I don't want to fight."

My hands clamped over her wrists and I pried her away. "No."

It wasn't the first time she'd made a pass at me since the divorce. Sex was her way of getting out of trouble, and during our marriage, it had worked. But never after we'd split.

"This is about that woman, the nanny, isn't it?" she sneered and stepped away.

"Natalie. Her name is Natalie. And you can get used to her being around." Because if I had my way, Natalie was going to be a familiar face in everyone's lives, Cece's included.

"How long have you and *Natalie* been fucking?"

"That's none of your business. And I'm done with this conversation. You can stay here tonight and tomorrow I'll expect you to find a hotel. You're welcome to visit Violet while you're here but you need to call first. If you take her anywhere, you need to tell me where you're going and how long you'll be gone."

She tossed her hands in the air. "You act like I'm a criminal."

"No, I'm acting like a parent. I've been the one to pick up Violet after you leave. I'm the one left holding her while she cries and deals with the fact that her mother doesn't give a shit about her life. So things are going to change. My daughter, my rules. You can either conform or get the fuck out. Understand?"

Her mouth fell open.

"Do. You. Understand?"

She blinked.

"I'll take that as a yes." Without another word, I walked to the door, whipping it open and holding it for her as she marched out of the office and down the hallway to find our daughter.

Thankfully, her irritation with me didn't bleed into her time with Violet. Cece managed to stow her frustration and act perfectly happy to shower Violet with hugs and kisses.

I spent the rest of the night hovering, watching as Violet showed her mother all of the Christmas presents she'd received. While Violet took her shower, I hauled up Cece's three suitcases to Violet's room because they'd decided to sleep in the same bed. Then after Violet was dressed in her pajamas and had brushed out her hair, I tucked her into bed.

"Good night, princess." I bent to kiss Violet's forehead and give her a hug. "I love you."

"Love you too, Daddy." She snuggled into her pillow.

I stood and glanced at Cece who was propped up on a bunch of pillows beside our daughter.

"Night, Mad."

"Night." I nodded, my heart twisting at the smile on my daughter's face.

Cece could be a good mother. When she tried, when she put her own selfishness aside, she could be a good mother. Violet adored her and craved her attention.

But Cece wasn't there enough. She never had been.

I walked out of the room, easing the door closed save for a small crack. Then I leaned in to listen.

"Did you know that we're moving here?" Violet asked Cece.

"That's what Daddy said. You like it here, don't you?"

"Yeah. It's pretty fun."

Yesterday, after the presents and Christmas meal, I'd sat Violet down and asked her if she'd be okay moving to Montana sooner than later. Though she'd been bummed to leave her friends, I'd promised she'd make new ones. And I'd promised that every Saturday, we'd go sledding.

Natalie had suggested we find a special activity. Sledding and swimming in the hot tub and whatever else we fit into our Saturdays would be our special activities.

"Can you move here too, Mommy?"

I held my breath, leaning in closer.

"I don't know if I can. Sorry."

"Oh," Violet murmured.

I rolled my eyes. It wasn't like there was a job keeping Cece in California.

"Should we go shopping tomorrow?" Cece asked.

"Sure." There was a rustle of covers as Violet shifted. Then an audible yawn—it was three hours past Violet's normal bedtime.

I inched away from the door, walking downstairs to where Mom was waiting in the living room with a full glass of wine.

"Where's Dad?" I asked.

"He went out to the hot tub."

I nodded and took a seat on the couch beside her, blowing out a long breath. "If she just tried . . . why can't she be like this every time?"

"I don't know, son."

"It breaks my heart. Because when she wants to be a mother, Violet adores her." I hadn't seen Violet this happy in weeks. Her smile. Her laugh. It was almost painful to witness because I knew it would all vanish when Cece did. "What do I do?"

"What you're doing." Mom put her hand on my knee. "Be there for Violet when she leaves."

"Christ, this is hard." I ran a hand over the stubble on my jaw. "How pissed is Dad?"

"Oh, he's pretty pissed. I expect him to disappear first thing in the morning like your brother did tonight. He's worried that if he is around Cece, he won't be able to keep his mouth shut."

Dad was the steady in the house. When Mom was angry, she let it blow. But not Dad. My family hated Cece and rightly so. Mom might be one to lose it, but Dad would simply steer clear and keep it to himself. On the rare occasion he did lose his temper, it was best to be out of the county.

"That would actually be fairly entertaining to see Dad lose it."

Mom laughed. "He rarely does, but I wouldn't want to be in her Jimmy Choos if he does."

"We were having such a good night."

"Yes, we were."

"I screwed up with Natalie. I shouldn't have let her leave." Maybe I should have kicked Cece out instead and made my choice crystal clear.

"No, it was right to talk with Cece alone."

Maybe. But I couldn't leave things with Natalie like this all night. She had to know that she was important too.

"Mom, I need to get some air." I stood from the couch. "Would you mind being here in case Violet needs anything?"

"I've got her. You go. And say hi to Natalie."

I grinned. "How'd you know I'm going to see Natalie?"

"Because I have three very smart sons. It's not easy to fit into the Holiday mix but Natalie does. Like she's always belonged."

Good to know I wasn't the only one who'd felt it.

Maybe it should have unsettled me, diving headfirst into a new relationship. After the disaster with Cece, I'd been hesitant to date. But not with Natalie. Every bone in my body vibrated with the need to be around her. To hold her close and see just where this was headed.

I bent down and kissed Mom's cheek. "Thanks."

"See you in the morning."

I hurried toward the garage, grabbing one of Dad's coats from the hook beside the door. Then I stepped into my shoes and hopped in the car, speeding across town for the dark green house and a woman who was quickly stealing my heart.

The lights were off except for a flicker of blue and white flashes through the front window from the TV. I knocked on the door, waiting in the cold as my breath billowed around me. Then the lock clicked open and there she stood, wearing a pair of Santa-print pajamas. Her hair was piled on top of her head in a messy bun. The makeup she'd had on earlier was gone.

She'd never looked more beautiful.

"Maddox?"

"I'm sorry."

"You drove across town to apologize?" She waved me inside. "You could have just called."

"No, I wanted to do this in person. I'm sorry that we didn't get our date. I'm sorry that the date we had was interrupted."

Her gaze softened. "I had fun."

"Still, that's not what I wanted. But what if we pretended?"

"Pretended what?"

"What if we pretended it was exactly as I'd planned? We went to dinner. I flattered you with my charm and kissed you good night at this door."

"Hmm." She hummed, a smile at the corner of her mouth. "You know, I'm not good with pretend. Maybe show me what you mean."

"Like this." I took her face in my hands and dropped my lips to hers, inhaling her sweet scent and savoring the softness of her lips.

She sank into my arms, opening her mouth for my tongue.

Just one taste, then I let her go. "About what Cece said. The nanny comment. It's not true. I've never been with one of Violet's nannies. Until you."

"I know."

"You do?"

"I trust you, Maddox. I believe *you*."

I'd been lucky in my life. With my family. My daughter. My career. Certain days stood apart from the others. Like the day last week when I'd opened the door to Natalie.

"I'm going to kiss you again."

"Hold that thought." She laced her fingers through mine and pulled me through the house, stopping at the living room to flip off the television. Then she tugged me down a hallway to her bedroom.

"Natalie." I stopped inside the doorway.

"I thought you were going to kiss me."

Oh, I was. Everywhere. "Before I do, I want you to know that I want this. You and me. I don't want to take it slow. I don't want to wait to be with you. But if you need time—"

"I don't." She walked over and slid her hands up my coat and to my shoulders. Then she shoved it off, the jacket landing with a thud by my feet.

I dove for her as she came at me, our lips smashing together. There was no hesitancy in this kiss, no reservation. I kissed her like I'd wanted to kiss her since that first time. A kiss that was just a prelude to what was to come.

She fumbled with the hem of my sweater, shoving it up my stomach. Then her hands came to my abs and she yanked her lips away.

"What?" I glanced down to where her hands were frozen on my skin.

She blushed and reached past me for the light switch, flooding the room in color. "No way we're doing this in the dark."

I chuckled and grabbed a fistful of my sweater and the T-shirt underneath, yanking them over my head.

Natalie's eyes went wide as they raked down my chest and to where my jeans sat low on my hips. "Hello, Maddox Holiday."

Every hour spent with my personal trainer in LA letting him torture me paid off with the flare in her eyes.

"Your turn." I unclasped the buttons of her pajama shirt one at a time, taking my time as I popped them apart. When I reached the last one, her breath was coming in short pants. My fingers grazed the creamy skin of her stomach and the small jewel that adorned her belly button. Then like she'd done with my coat, I shoved the top off those pretty shoulders.

My arms flew around her, hauling her into my chest. Those rosy, pebbled nipples grazed my skin as I shoved at the waistband of her bottoms.

Her fingers worked the zipper on my jeans but I kept them on, even though my cock ached to slide inside her tight, delicious body. If she wanted an orgasm with the lights on, I was all for it. I could stare at her long, toned legs and sexy curves for days and not have my fill.

I dropped my lips to her neck, sucking below her ear, then I fell to my knees.

Her fingers threaded through my hair as I took in her bare mound.

"Nat." I placed a kiss below her navel.

"Maddox." My name on her lips was the best gift I'd had in years.

I leaned in and dragged my tongue across her folds, her sweetness exploding in my mouth.

Natalie's hands tightened in my hair, the sting in my scalp all the encouragement I needed to do it again.

Sliding one hand up the inside of her leg, I found her wet center and plunged a finger inside. She shuddered as I sucked and licked and fucked her with my tongue until she shouted my name and nearly collapsed as the first orgasm washed over her.

Her limbs trembled with the aftershocks of her release

as I picked her up and carried her to the bed, whipping back the covers and settling her on the cool sheets. Then I went back to the light switch, bathing the room in darkness.

It was going to kill me to walk out of here.

I went to her side and kissed her forehead. "Good night."

"Ni—wait. What?" She shoved up on her elbows. "Where are you going?"

"I don't have a condom." So I was going home for a cold, cold shower. Maybe I'd just jump in a snowbank.

"Oh." The disappointment on her face made the sting of blue balls pinch a little less. "I haven't been with anyone in over a year. And I'm on birth control."

"It's been longer for me."

She shoved the covers aside and smiled, her hands drifting up her flat stomach to her nipples where she pinched them between her fingers.

I groaned and stripped out of my jeans, my cock, aching and hard, springing free. I wrapped a hand around the shaft and stroked before climbing into her bed and settling into the cradle of her hips.

She kissed me, not caring that her taste was still on my lips.

And when I slid inside, my eyes locked with hers, I knew this was the Christmas that was going to change everything.

CHAPTER ELEVEN

NATALIE

"That was . . ." I panted, trying to regain my breath. Two orgasms and I was wrecked.

Maddox had collapsed beside me, his chest rising and falling as my heart thundered. "Fuck, I'm never leaving this bed."

"Good plan." I smiled as he yanked me into his side, holding me tight. I draped an arm over his abs, drawing circles in the dusting of hair on his chest as we both regained our breath. "So what happened with your ex?"

He shifted, propping his head up with an arm as the other kept me pinned to his side. "Probably something that should have happened years ago. I wasn't nice."

"Eeek."

"She needed to hear it. Cece can step up or step out. But I'm done pandering to her."

"Good. And how is Violet?"

"I love that you ask about my daughter." He kissed my hair. "She's good. She loves Cece, despite it all."

"And she will. Until she's older."

"I'm sorry that you had to go through that with your mother."

I leaned up and put my chin on his chest so I could see his face. "It used to bother me. I'd get so mad, especially when I was a teenager, but every year I think about her less and less. The anger fades. The resentment. And I have Judy. I wouldn't trade her for anything in the world."

Judy was ten times the mother that my real mother had been. And even though not having a mom for most of my life had been difficult at times, Dad had been enough.

The two of us had simply been waiting for Judy.

Maddox leaned forward, brushing a kiss to my lips. "We need to talk."

"Uh-oh."

"A good talk." He twisted fast, forcing me to my back. Then he hovered over me, his hands tangling in my hair. "What do you say we lean into this? Lean hard."

"What do you mean?"

"It seems crazy that we've only known each other for days. It feels like longer."

"I was thinking that tonight too when we were playing games." Like I'd always been there. Maybe the Holiday crew was simply welcoming, but we'd all clicked so effortlessly that there hadn't been a single awkward moment.

"Good. Because I have an idea and I need you to hear me out."

"Okay," I drawled.

"I don't want to hire another nanny. Violet needs me around, and I'm willing to admit that when I have a nanny, I rely too much on someone else's help. That said, I have to work. It's her legacy I'm building. She'll have every opportunity in the world because of my company, and selfishly, I don't want to give up Madcast. It's my dream. We've got a long way to grow and I want to be there."

"You shouldn't give it up." He'd built it and he should have the chance to see it flourish.

"My job isn't a nine-to-five," he said. "I need some help with Violet and as much as I love my parents, they've already raised their kids. I'm not putting this on them either. I hope you won't be mad, but earlier tonight before Cathy left, I asked her what you have coming."

"You did?"

He nodded. "She said you're going to work for another family starting in January."

"That was the plan. Until today."

"What do you mean? What happened today?"

I blew out a long breath. "I've been thinking of making some changes too. It's time to stop stalling. I don't want to be a nanny my entire life. I want to get my degree and become a therapist. It might take me twenty years because I'll probably need to work part-time too. But it's time."

"Then this could work." The excitement on his face

was contagious and I smiled before he even pitched this idea. "Be ours. Or friend. Or girlfriend. Whatever you want to call us. Just be ours. Mine. Violet's. We'll work everything around your school schedule. But I want to see you every day. And I want Violet to see you every day."

Maybe it was crazy to jump this far into a commitment with a man I didn't know very well. Or maybe it would be crazy to push him away.

Dad had met Judy, and in only two weeks, he'd married her. When I'd asked him why he hadn't dated her longer, he'd told me it was because he already knew. They'd both known instantly. And neither had wanted to delay the start of their life together.

Things were different with Maddox and me. Violet wasn't a twenty-year-old woman with a job. She was much younger, and for her, we'd have to take it slower.

But this idea . . .

"Girlfriend," I said. "I don't want to be the nanny. I don't want to be paid. I don't want anything but to see you every day. Violet too."

Maddox moved so fast I'd barely finished my sentence when his mouth crushed mine.

I ran my hands down his spine until my palms squeezed into the curve of his ass. The honed muscle might as well have been carved from stone.

He pressed into my side, his cock hardening between us as his spicy, heady, dizzying scent surrounded me. "I want you. Not just for tonight."

"I want you too." This was happening so fast but I didn't want to slow down. I was diving into Maddox, stroke after stroke, swimming toward the deep end of the ocean.

"Natalie," he whispered into my ear as he shifted, dragging his erection through my center before rocking inside.

I wrapped my arms around his strong back, feeling the muscles bunch beneath my hands. I spread my legs wider, circling his hips as my body stretched around him. My God, he was addicting. It shouldn't be this good so soon. It felt as if we'd been lovers for years, decades, not an hour.

"You feel so good, Nat." He pulled out only to slide inside again. Maddox's hands drifted down my ribs, his touch dragging sparks across my skin. He skimmed my hips and my thighs. He gripped the backs of my knees, pressing me apart as he came up onto his knees, staring down at me.

Our gazes locked as he thrust forward, hitting that place inside that made my toes curl. Move after move, he worked us together, his hips like pistons, until my legs were shaking and I writhed beneath him, a slave to his stamina.

"Maddox, I'm—" The words died on my tongue as the orgasm raced through my body, consuming every inch. Stars broke in my eyes and I cried out, surrendering to the man who was turning my life inside out.

"Fuck," Maddox hissed as I pulsed around his length.

My orgasm loosened its hold enough that I managed to crack my eyes open in time to see Maddox squeeze his shut and surrender to his own release on a groan.

I could watch this every freaking day and twice on Sunday. His muscles glistened with sweat as he poured himself inside of me. His handsome face barely illuminated from the window's muted light.

But he was mine.

Tonight, Maddox Holiday was mine.

Maybe this was fast. Maybe it was reckless and a little crazy. But there was something here. Something powerful and something worth holding on to.

Something to chase.

Maddox collapsed onto the bed, wrapping me in his arms. His heartbeat hammered against my own, his breaths a short staccato against the skin of my neck.

And I clung to him, not wanting him to let go. Not yet.

"Maddox." My voice shook as I breathed his name. From the orgasm. From the wave of emotion crashing over us both.

He leaned back, our bodies still connected, and met my gaze. His fingertips brushed the hair from my face. "What?"

"Do you feel this?"

"Yeah, Nat. I feel it."

I smiled, swallowing the lump in my throat. Shoving aside tears of joy as I leaned up and kissed him.

Maddox Holiday.

The boy who'd been my crush.

The man who'd win my love.

———

"I'LL SEE YOU LATER." Maddox dropped a kiss to my lips. "Give me until nine."

"Are you sure this is a good idea?" Dealing with Cece was inevitable but I was hoping to avoid it for a while longer.

"She'll be gone." He kissed me again.

"Okay. Bye." I stood in the doorway, the cold seeping through my pajamas, but I wanted to watch him drive away. So I clutched my coffee mug, shivering, and waiting until he waved from the driver's seat of his SUV and pulled away from the curb.

It was still dark outside at four in the morning, but Maddox had wanted to leave early so that Violet wouldn't catch him coming home and wonder where he'd slept last night.

The moment his taillights disappeared around the block, I retreated to the warmth of my house. I settled on my couch and turned on the TV. I went straight for the Madcast app to re-watch the most recent season of *State of Ruin*.

Five minutes into my episode, I went in search of my phone. I doubted he was home yet, but I texted Maddox anyway.

What are the chances I can get early access to State of Ruin's last season?

He didn't type a reply but, a second later, my phone vibrated in my hand.

"Is this why you're sleeping with me?" he asked.

"Who slept?" He'd woken me twice for sex and we'd done it again this morning before he'd climbed out of bed and dressed in yesterday's clothes.

"Good point." He chuckled. "I'll send you the login info if you keep it a secret."

"Yes." I fist-pumped. "Are you home?"

"Just about."

"Okay. See you in a bit."

"Bye, babe."

I smiled, hung up and snuggled under a blanket as I waited for the sun to rise so I could make my next phone call.

Actually, two phone calls.

My stomach was in a knot, the dread making me sick, but at promptly eight o'clock, I dialed Cathy's number.

"Tell me that you've changed your mind and you'll be going to watch Violet Holiday today."

"I'm going to go watch Violet Holiday today."

"Phew." She blew out a long breath. "She's a sweet girl but it's been a long time since I've had to entertain a seven-year-old. It was exhausting."

I smiled, loving that Violet had taken it easy on Cathy yesterday.

"What made you change your mind?" she asked.

"Do you want the good news or the bad news first?"

"No. Oh, Natalie. No."

"I'll finish out my week with Violet, but please consider this my resignation. I'm going to go to school."

The other end of the line was quiet for a long moment. Then she sighed. "I knew this call was coming. You're too smart and too driven to do this job forever. But I just hate to lose you."

My eyes flooded. I always cried at endings. "I'm sorry for the short notice."

"No, it's fine. You're in between families and this gives me time to juggle before you were supposed to start with the new family in January."

"Thank you, Cathy. For everything."

"Same to you, Natalie. Let's meet for coffee soon."

"I'd like that."

I hung up the phone, wishing I felt lighter. But quitting a job I'd had for years to start school was a fear of its own. What if I hated it? What if I failed?

What if I didn't?

The physical therapist I worked with in town had always encouraged me to consider school. He knew I loved being in the pool. Swimming had become a hobby as a kid, my dad taking me whenever he'd had a free minute in the summers. Then I'd become a lifeguard in high school and captained the swim team.

It would take me years to get my undergraduate degree, and that was only the beginning.

But today felt like the right first step.

It was time to say goodbye to nannying. Time to pursue a dream.

Time to let go of the past.

Which brought me to my next phone call.

"Hi, this is Natalie Buchanan," I said to the receptionist at the garage where Magdalena was being fixed. "This is going to seem strange since I was so anxious to get her fixed, but . . . I need to sell my bus."

CHAPTER TWELVE

MADDOX

Violet shuffled into my bathroom, her hair mussed and her eyelids heavy.

"Morning, sweetie."

She yawned as I picked her up and set her beside my sink. Then I went back to shaving, half of my face still covered in shaving cream.

There were two scratches on my shoulder from Natalie's nails. Having just come from the shower, I was only wearing a towel around my waist so I pivoted, not wanting Violet to ask how I'd gotten the marks.

"Why were you whistling?" she asked.

"Oh." I hadn't realized I'd been whistling. "I don't know. I guess I'm just in a good mood."

A damn good mood.

Last night with Natalie had been the best night I'd had in years. Sex, phenomenal sex, was part of it. But the other part of my good mood was just . . . Natalie. She made me happy.

"I like it when you whistle." Violet yawned again and gave me a sleepy smile.

"Me too." I finished shaving, rinsed my face and patted it dry. Then I left Violet, content on the counter, and went to the closet to get dressed.

In a pair of jeans and a simple gray sweater, I collected my daughter, taking her to the bedroom where the bed was still made from yesterday.

After I'd gotten home from Natalie's, I'd spent an hour in the office, not wanting to wash her scent off my body quite yet. Then when I'd suspected Violet would be waking up soon, I'd hurried through a shower.

"I need to talk to you about something," I said, sitting beside her.

Her shoulders stiffened. "What?"

"It's about Natalie. She's going to come back and hang out with you today."

"Okay." She relaxed. "What about Mommy? She said we could go shopping."

"And you can." When—if—Cece followed through, I'd have a little alone time with Natalie. "But Natalie is going to be around a lot more."

"As my nanny?"

I shook my head. "No. As my girlfriend."

Violet dropped her eyes to her lap, her fingers tugging at her cotton pajamas.

"How do you feel about that?"

She lifted a shoulder. "What about Mommy?"

"Your mom will always be your mom." There was an unspoken message there, one that Violet didn't miss. Cece wouldn't change, something Violet was beginning to understand.

My daughter was too smart for her own good at times.

"Mom doesn't make you whistle."

"No, she doesn't." I took one of Violet's hands and pressed it between mine.

"I like Natalie," she whispered.

"Me too. Want to take her on a date tonight?"

"I can go too?"

I nodded. "Just the three of us."

"What if Mommy is still here?"

"She can hang out with you for a while today. But she's going to be sleeping at a hotel tonight. And while I'm working, Natalie will be here. Then we'll go to dinner."

If Cece surprised me and entertained Violet all day, I'd be shocked. Hence why Natalie was coming over because I was betting that we'd need backup.

"Okay. Can I have breakfast?"

"Sure." I kissed her hair and led her to the hall. We passed her room and I glanced inside, not seeing Cece. Her suitcase was open on the floor and the bed was unmade. "Where is your mom?"

"She was getting some coffee."

I was surprised that Cece had let Violet out of her

sight. Not because she'd missed her, but because Cece was in enemy territory. I'd assumed she would have used Violet as a shield around my parents.

The house was quiet as we made our way to the kitchen. The door was closed to Mom's office. I'd heard the garage door open and close earlier. That had probably been Dad disappearing to Holiday Homes.

I'd send them both an all-clear text later once Cece was gone.

Violet and I found Cece in the kitchen, sitting at the island with a steaming mug of coffee. She was dressed in a pair of jeans and a turtleneck. Her hair was perfectly styled and her makeup artfully applied.

"Morning," I said.

"Hi." She barely looked at me, but smiled at Violet. "Would you like breakfast?"

"No, thanks."

"Suit yourself." I went to the pantry, smirking that I'd kissed Natalie here last night.

Violet chose cereal and I set her up beside Cece at the island.

Other than Violet's crunching, silence consumed the kitchen, awkward and tense. Cece refused to make eye contact. I poured my own cup of coffee and watched my daughter eat, the occasional dribble of milk dripping down her chin.

When she was finished, I took her bowl and put it in

the dishwasher. "Can you go get dressed? I need to talk to your mom for a few minutes. Grown-ups only."

Violet frowned but obeyed, trudging from the room. Her footsteps paused past the first wall.

"Violet," I warned.

"Fine." She huffed and this time she actually obeyed.

"How was your night?" Cece's teeth ground together when she finally looked at me.

"Good."

"Is it really appropriate for you to leave Violet in the middle of the night to visit your nanny?"

"Natalie," I corrected, keeping my voice even. "And I don't think you get to talk to me about what is and is not appropriate, considering you used to fuck Rip in my bed."

Her eyes narrowed.

"I didn't notice a car outside. Would you like me to order you an Uber to take you to a hotel?"

"If you're going to be disappearing every night, then maybe Violet should stay with me there."

"Absolutely not. You can take her shopping today if you'd like, but I expect her back by five. We have plans tonight."

"You made plans? I rarely get to see her. You're taking her away from California. I fly all the way up here and you make plans?"

There was so much I could tackle in her statement. So much to throw in her face. But I'd said it all before and it hadn't mattered. It wouldn't now. "Yes, we have plans."

"Unbelievable. I'll be back for Violet before lunch." She huffed and slid off her seat, marching out of the kitchen, but before she could disappear, I called her name.

"Cece."

"What?" She spun around and crossed her arms.

"Natalie will be here today. She's important to me. She's important to Violet. I expect you to show her the same respect I've shown your boyfriend, and by that, I mean you need to keep your mouth shut."

"Seriously?"

"I'm glad we understand each other."

With a hair flip and an eye roll, she disappeared, leaving me in the empty room.

I shook my head, rubbing at the ache forming behind a temple. It was never easy with her. But I was giving Cece a day and then I suspected she'd be gone. She'd throw her temper tantrum and fly home.

My phone vibrated in my pocket like it had been all morning and I was sure that a string of emails and voice-mails would greet me when I got to my desk. But all of that was going to have to wait until Cece was gone and Natalie was here. Where she belonged.

Last night had been the turning point. Like I'd warned her, I wasn't going to wait. I wasn't taking this slow.

Maybe it was foolish, given my history with Cece, but my gut screamed that Natalie was the one. It was the same feeling I'd had when I'd started Madcast. It was the same feeling I had when someone pitched a hit show.

I knew.

Soul deep.

I took out my phone and pulled up her name, hitting the screen.

"Hi," she answered with a sniffle that made me stand straighter.

"What's wrong?"

"Nothing," she said, too brightly. "Still want me to come over and hang out with Violet?"

"If you're up for it."

"Of course." Another sniffle.

"Nat, what's wrong?"

She blew out a long breath. "I quit my job. And I gave up Magdalena."

"Magdalena?"

"My 1969 mint-green Volkswagen bus. She's been at the mechanic, and I realized this morning if I'm going to pay for school, I need a vehicle that doesn't require specialty parts when she's broken down."

"You named your car Magdalena."

"Um . . . yes. Don't you name your cars?"

"No." But it didn't surprise me in the least that she did. "Do you want to stay home today?"

"I'll be fine. A lot is changing."

"For the better?"

"For the best," she whispered. "Don't worry about me. I'm good. See you soon."

"Bye." I refilled my coffee, then lingered outside of

Violet's room as Cece packed her luggage. I hauled her suitcases to the front door and waited for her Uber to arrive. She promised to be back by eleven, which meant noon.

Not ten minutes after Cece left, Natalie pulled up in her Subaru.

"So who is that?" I asked, motioning to the car as she came inside the foyer.

"My dad's. He loaned it to me. He doesn't name his cars either, but I'm considering calling him Barney."

I chuckled and pulled her into my arms. "Hi."

"Hi." She melted into me, rising on her toes as I brought my lips down to hers. The kiss wasn't long enough, and if Cece showed up like she'd promised, I'd ignore whatever was on my calendar and take Natalie to my bedroom.

We tore ourselves apart, both turning to freeze at the blue eyes waiting.

Violet had definitely been watching as I'd kissed Natalie.

My daughter studied us, her eyes darting back and forth, then she smiled at Natalie. "Can we play with my Christmas presents?"

"Absolutely." Natalie whipped off her coat, winked at me and let my daughter steal her away.

I went to my office with a smile on my face.

It only lasted through the morning.

Because by noon, when Cece was supposed to be back

for Violet, I received a text that her plans had changed and she'd already hopped on a plane for California.

"Fuck." My curse echoed through my office.

I shouldn't have been surprised. With my attitude yesterday and today, I'd pissed her off. Add in Natalie, and it wasn't a shock that Cece had chosen to leave rather than deal with circumstances like an adult in order to spend time with her child.

But it had never been about Violet. Cece was uncomfortable and therefore she was gone.

And I'd be the one to deliver the news to my girl.

I found Natalie and Violet in the kitchen, raiding the fridge. The chef had his earbuds in, chopping herbs on the opposite end, as far from Violet as possible. He kept one eye on her, another on his knife.

"Hi, Daddy." Violet looked past me as I strode into the room, probably wondering if Cece was here.

"We were just going to make sandwiches for lunch, keep it simple." The smile on Natalie's face faded when she noted my expression. "What happened?"

I nodded to Violet, my heart breaking.

Natalie's shoulders fell.

"Violet, I need to talk to you, princess."

"Why?" She studied my face for a long moment. Then her chin began to quiver. "Mom left, didn't she?"

Fucking Cece. I wouldn't forgive her for this. For any of it. How could she not take one look at Violet and see an amazing little girl who just wanted to be loved?

"Yeah. She left."

The first tear fell down Violet's cheek and I opened my arms.

But she didn't turn to me. She turned to Natalie.

"I'm sorry, Violet." Natalie closed the fridge and knelt beside my daughter.

The first sob escaped Violet's mouth and then she flew into Natalie's arms, clinging to her as she cried. "I hate her. I hate her! She didn't even bring me a Christmas present."

Natalie wrapped her up tight and closed her eyes, stroking Violet's hair. "I'm sorry."

Hearing Violet cry was too much, so I walked over, dropped down, and held them both.

It took Violet a while to stop, but when she did, we let her go and I wiped the tears off her cheeks. "I love you."

"I love you too," she whispered, her tiny mouth turned down.

"Let's have some lunch. Then we'll have fun the rest of the day." I'd call my assistant and tell him to cancel my meetings for the rest of the week. I needed to spend time with my daughter. And I wanted Natalie with us.

"What kind of fun?" Violet asked.

"I thought we could drive out and look at the place where we're going to build our house. Then maybe we could go sledding. Or to a movie."

"Sledding," Natalie and Violet said in unison.

So we went sledding. Afterward, we drove past our

new property and Violet squealed when she saw the pond. Then we went to a movie, just the three of us.

In a way, it felt like the first day of our new life.

"Who's hungry?" I asked as we left the theater.

"Me." Violet and Natalie both raised their hands. They'd eaten an entire tub of popcorn and a bag of M&M's.

"Okay, we need to make one more stop, then we can go to dinner."

"Where are we going?" Violet asked.

"You'll see." I winked, taking her hand.

Violet grabbed Natalie with her other and we swung her between us while Natalie looked over with those beautiful blue eyes and breathtaking smile.

"Thank you," I mouthed.

If not for her, I don't think Violet would have recovered so quickly from Cece's disappointment today. As we'd driven around town, bouncing between activities, Violet had asked Natalie questions about her own mother. How old she'd been when she'd left. How many Christmas presents Natalie's mom had forgotten to give her.

For Violet, knowing that she wasn't alone in this seemed to help her cope.

Natalie had mentioned Judy a few times throughout the day, and each time Violet would look to me and smile.

Mom had said last night that Natalie fit.

I knew it.

So did my daughter.

Natalie was Violet's Judy.

We piled into the car and drove away from the theater, heading across town.

"Where are we going?" Natalie asked.

"I was going to buy you some flowers for our first date."

"Aww." She smiled. "That's sweet."

I grinned and kept on driving.

During the movie, I'd excused myself under the ruse of refilling the popcorn and using the bathroom. Really, I'd swiped Natalie's phone so I could call her father.

After a quick introduction, I'd asked him if he knew about Magdalena.

Garrett had told me everything, about how the bus had been Natalie's mother's, and despite his hatred of that vehicle, Nat had always loved it. His voice had been so loud and deep that I'd had to listen with the phone an inch from my ear.

He'd given me the mechanic's name and number, and I'd told Garrett we'd meet soon. Then I'd made another call.

"Where are we going?" Natalie sat straighter in her seat, recognizing the street I turned down. This part of Bozeman was made up of industrial buildings and a lumberyard.

Not a flower shop in sight.

"Like I said, I was going to buy you flowers but I had a better idea." I slowed and pulled into the garage's small lot, parking in front of the first bay door. When I'd spoken to the owner, he'd promised to stick around until we arrived. "We're going to rescue Magdalena."

"Maddox." Natalie pressed her hands to her cheeks. "This is too much."

I shook my head. "Let me do this."

"Maddox—"

"Consider it your Christmas present. From Violet and me."

"No. It's too much. Way too much."

"Do you love Magdalena?"

"Who's Magdalena?" Violet asked from the backseat.

"My car," Natalie answered.

"Your car is named Magdalena? Daddy, why doesn't our car have a name?"

"Well, this is a rental. I don't know if you name rental cars."

"You can," Natalie said.

"Okay, then we'll just have to come up with one. You can pick."

"James," Violet declared with a nod.

"I like it." Natalie reached back for a fist bump. "What about a middle name?"

Before Violet could answer, I held up a hand. "How about you introduce us to Magdalena, I'll pay for whatever repairs she needs, then you two can discuss a middle name for James over dinner?"

Natalie sighed. "You can't pay for Magdalena to get fixed."

"It's happening, babe." Eventually she'd get used to lavish gifts because there were many in her future. "Come on."

She opened her door and moved to the back to help Violet out, and then we met with the shop owner. And met Magdalena.

The bus screamed Natalie. The moment I spotted it, I knew I'd do whatever was necessary so she could drive that bus for as long as she wanted.

I thanked the mechanic, who assured me that he'd have the new parts installed soon, and Magdalena would be as good as new in a couple of weeks.

With that settled, I loaded Violet and Natalie into *James* and drove us to dinner. We talked about everything over a large supreme pizza. Natalie's favorite foods. Violet's favorite movies. My favorite part of the day.

This.

Our first date.

The best first date of my life.

With any luck, the last first date.

"Thank you for coming in," the waitress said as she delivered our check to the booth.

Behind her, another waitress walked by carrying a skillet heaped with ice cream.

Natalie and Violet shared a look.

Kindred sweet tooths.

I held up a hand before the waitress could set down the bill, then pointed to the dessert. "We're going to need one of those."

Natalie cleared her throat.

"Make that two."

EPILOGUE
NATALIE

O *ne year later ...*
      "Dance with me." Maddox took my hand,
rescuing me from the group of ladies who'd surrounded
me and dragged me into a conversation about water births.

"Yes, please." I followed him through the crowd,
squeezing past clusters of partygoers.

This year's Holiday Christmas party was packed. If I'd
thought last year's party had been busy, the ballroom was
practically bursting at its seams. Probably because it
wasn't on Christmas Eve.

Most of the faces in the crowd were unfamiliar, even
though there were plenty of friends and family here too.

Dad and Judy were at the bar. Judy's cheeks were red
and her smile bright. Dad was the designated driver
tonight and Judy was into the champagne.

She spotted me and waved just as Violet raced up to

them, taking Dad's hand and pulling him toward the dance floor.

Maddox swung me into his arms, holding me close.

"Who called you?" I asked. He'd stepped away a few minutes ago to answer his phone.

"Cece," he muttered.

I stiffened. "What did she want?"

"She wants to come up on Monday to see Violet. We'll see if she actually shows up."

"I don't think we should tell Violet."

"Yeah, I was thinking that too. If Cece shows, it will be a surprise. If she doesn't, Violet will never know."

We'd learned our lesson the last time Cece had called and announced she was coming to Montana for a visit.

Our beautiful girl had sat by the front window, watching the driveway for hours and waiting for her mother to show. Finally, worried that something had happened, Maddox had called Cece only to find out she'd changed her plans last minute. She'd given him some excuse about the weather and flying conditions.

I suspected it was because before her flight, Cece had called Violet who'd slipped and told her that I was pregnant.

Maybe ditching Violet was her way of punishing us. Whatever her reasons, Cece hadn't changed and I doubted she ever would. She came and went whenever it suited her, which wasn't often. And when she broke

Violet's heart, Maddox and I were there to pick up the pieces.

I leaned into his broad chest, smiling as his hand drifted to the small of my back. The song was a fast one, but the two of us danced to our own rhythm.

There was barely any space to move anyway. This close to midnight, the floor was full of happy, drunken adults.

"Violet's having fun," I said, finding her and Dad in the crowd. "And she looks so pretty tonight."

When we'd gone to a small shop downtown to pick out a dress, I'd let her choose. I'd assumed she'd go with her standard red, but as we'd perused the racks, she'd chosen a velvet green dress that swished at her knees.

Like last year, Hannah had bought her a tiara.

"She does." Maddox glanced over at his daughter, then bent and kissed my neck. "You look beautiful."

He'd told me the same countless times tonight. My fitted gray dress molded to my baby bump. The diamond earrings he'd bought me as an early Christmas gift were my only adornment, except for my wedding rings.

Just like we'd decided last year, Maddox and I hadn't waited.

We'd started this life together without delay and not a day had passed when I'd regretted a single moment.

After Christmas last year, I'd enrolled at Montana State, adjusting my class schedule so I could pick Violet up from school every day. Maddox had given his father and brothers the green light to build his house and the day it was finished, we'd all moved in together.

We'd been dating for six months at that point. The week after we'd moved in, Maddox and I had gotten married. The ceremony had been simple. I'd worn a fitted white gown. He'd opted for a black suit. And with Violet as our flower girl, we'd stood beside the pond in our yard and exchanged vows with our family and close friends watching on.

One week later, I'd realized that the reason my stomach had been in a constant state of tornado hadn't been because of wedding stress. But because I was pregnant.

When I'd showed him the positive test, Maddox had let out a whoop so loud the ducks in the pond had flown away. We'd talked about a baby—it was just happening sooner than planned.

But we both wanted Violet to have a sibling. I loved being her stepmom, and though a baby might delay my education for a while, I didn't mind. Someday, I'd be a therapist. In the meantime, I was going to enjoy time with my family.

"Are you having fun?" I asked my husband as we danced.

"Yeah. You?"

I hummed my agreement just as someone bumped into my butt. "Yes, but your parents are going to have to find a bigger venue."

Maddox chuckled. "Mom said the same thing earlier."

"I love you," I said, yawning and leaning on Maddox's shoulder.

"I love you too."

He moved us around the dance floor, holding me tight. He did the same when we were at home. He'd come up behind me and twirl me into his arms, dancing me around the bedroom while he stripped me out of my clothes.

Maddox had a way of balancing naughty and nice, and I thanked the universe every day that I'd been called to be his nanny.

THREE BELLS, TWO BOWS AND ONE BROTHER'S BEST FRIEND

I pride myself in being grounded. Sure, I've had my share of childhood fantasies. Winning an Oscar. Winning the lottery. Winning an Olympic medal for an athletic talent I have yet to discover. But the only fantasy I ever thought might actually happen was winning my brother's best friend.

Heath Holiday.

My crush on him has ebbed and flowed over the years, but the day I started working for his construction company was the day I smothered it for good. Sort of. Mostly. It was on my to-do list. Making it a priority would have been easier had he not arrived at his family's annual Christmas party looking ridiculously handsome in a suit.

Then he kissed me. We stepped into an alternate universe and he kissed me. I assumed the next day I'd just be Guy's little sister again. The office newbie. Our kiss forgotten. Except he keeps showing up at my house. With gifts.

A gold bracelet carrying three jingling bells. Two dainty jeweled earrings, each shaped as a bow. And finally, he brought himself.

One brother's best friend, asking if I can keep a secret.

A PARTRIDGE AND A PREGNANCY

There are a lot of places I'd rather spend Christmas Eve morning than on a cold, snowy sidewalk outside someone else's home. I'd kill to be sitting beside a fireplace, drinking cocoa, wearing flannel pajamas and reading a book.

Instead, I'm here, standing in front of my one-night stand's house, working up the courage to ring the doorbell and tell him I'm pregnant.

I hate that term—one-night stand. It sounds so cheap and sleezy. Tobias Holiday is neither of those things. He's handsome and caring. Witty and charismatic. And once, a long time ago, he was mine.

Our one-night reunion was only supposed to be a hookup. A fling with an old lover. A parting farewell before I moved to London and put my feelings for him an ocean away. How exactly am I supposed to explain that to

Tobias that I'm having a baby? His baby? Maybe I could sing it. He always loved the silly songs I made up in the shower.

Three French hens, two turtle doves.

And a partridge and a pregnancy.

ACKNOWLEDGMENTS

Happy Holidays! I hope this book was as fun for you to read as it was for me to write. On a whim, I decided last Christmas to write three stories for this Christmas. I dragged it out over the course of months because that Christmas cheer was such a joy to add to my every day.

A huge thanks to my editing and proofreading team: Marion, Karen, Judy and Julie. Thank you to Sarah Hansen for the cutest covers in the world. Thanks to my agent, Kimberly, and the team at Brower Literary. And my publicist, Nina, and the team at Valentine PR.

Thanks to the members of Perry and Nash. I'm not sure how I got so lucky to have such an incredible reader group for both my Devney Perry and my Willa Nash books, but know that your love and support mean the world to me.

The same is true for the amazing bloggers who read and promote my stories. I am so grateful for you all!

And lastly, thanks to Bill, Will and Nash. I wrote these books in the evenings and love that you let me take an hour here and there to play with these characters.

ABOUT THE AUTHOR

Willa Nash is *USA Today* Bestselling Author Devney Perry's alter ego, writing contemporary romance stories for Kindle Unlimited. Lover of Swedish Fish, hater of laundry, she lives in Washington State with her husband and two sons. She was born and raised in Montana and has a passion for writing books in the state she calls home.

Don't miss out on Willa's latest book news.
Subscribe to her newsletter!
www.willanash.com

Made in the USA
Columbia, SC
28 October 2021

47583891R00126